THE HUR YOCHA

For my mum Millie thank you for everything

This book is a work of fiction. Names, characters, organisations, places, events and incidents are either products of the author's imagination or are used fictitiously.

Visit my web site for all the latest books and news.

www.colingaltrey.co.uk

THE HURT OF YOCHANA

Can things like this really happen?

Remember **"LOOKING FOR SHONA"**

THE HURT OF YOCHANA is a book about Jane Egan daughter of Liam and Joan Egan and the similarities that cross from her parent's lives to Jane's.

Is it Time Travel, is it a Treasured Gift or is it possession by an unknown person?

You decide!!

THE HURT OF
YOCHANA

Jamie sat and with tears in his eyes he turned to Millie.

"That's it then, Jane is off to University." "Hey don't be daft we can go up and see her she is only in Liverpool Jamie."

"Might as well be a million miles away she will grow away from us now Millie." Jamie had always been very protective of Jane, all through the years Liam had been poorly she was more like a daughter to him he idolised her.

"She isn't our daughter Jamie."

"She is as good as. There is nothing I would not do for that girl Millie, she is my best friend's daughter, sorry **our** best friend's daughter." Millie felt quite bad they had discovered a month earlier that she could not have children. Jamie had been understanding but she knew it had

been his dream to have his own children.
As they were talking, suddenly there was a
tap on the window. It was Jane.

"I saw you hadn't gone yet, shall we
have a quick drink? There is a nice coffee
shop I have just seen." Jane was a kind girl
and she knew Jamie was finding this hard.
They locked the car and walked the three
hundred yards to the coffee shop. Jane
linked arms with Jamie and Millie could
see him beaming as they entered the
coffee shop.

"Three coffees please." The kindly
gentleman placed a small menu in front of
them.

"We are famous in Liverpool, my
mother makes the best cheesecake. All the
students come here. We once had Ringo
Star come to the coffee shop with his wife,

the Bond girl," and he pointed to a stained picture on the wall.

"Well tell you what, if Ringo likes your Mum's cheesecake we best have some my man. I will have chocolate despair, what about you Millie?"

"Oh let me see. I'll have Mango and Pineapple please. Come on Jane surprise us."

"I'm going to have the Jewish Cheesecake." The man smiled and in his best Jewish voice said, "You will be blessed my dear."

"So is this a Jewish café then Jane?"

"Not sure, it's the first time I have been in. When I came up to look round I never went down this street. What a lovely man." The Cheesecakes arrived and a very old lady brought Jane's over to her. "

"This is my mother, Maria Klinck. She

THE HURT OF
YOCHANA

is ninety three years old. She was born in nineteen twenty three and she survived the holocaust." Jamie, Millie and Jane all stood up and hugged Maria who was as sharp as a knife and her stature belied her years.

"Thank you," she said and she went back into the kitchen but said something to her son.

"She wants to see you before you go," he said to Jane.

"See you are special Jane. I always told your Mum and Dad that."

"You are biased Uncle Jamie." She had always called them Aunty and Uncle.

"This cheesecake is something else, we are definitely coming here the next time we come to visit Jane." They finished their coffee and cheesecake and paid the bill Maria came out from the kitchen and gave

THE HURT OF YOCHANA

Jane a plastic flower she then whispered in her ear.

As they left Millie asked Jane what the older lady had said.

"It was a bit strange. She said look after this gift and the gift will look after you. She said never forget and remember I am here for you."

"That's odd, she didn't know you until today, did she Jane?"

"I know."

"Well you best put the rose safe then and look after it," and they all laughed.

Jane kissed them goodbye for the second time and said she was going to come to London in a month's time but she would e- mail them.

"You better lady, and not too much partying you hear."

THE HURT OF
YOCHANA

"Flippin' heck listen to that Aunty Millie. That coming from the oldest swinger in town, lecturing a mere child on the dangers of partying. My dad told me all about your legendary dance moves Uncle Jamie," and she laughed as she flung her brown scarf Aunty Millie had knitted for her as a going away present, over her shoulder and skipped down the street.

"You feel better now don't you Jamie?"

"I know its silly Millie, but the world is such a horrible place these days and I can't help but worry."

"I understand but we have to let her live her life and flourish Jamie."

"I know and I am trying honestly." As they drove back to London Millie saw Jamie was deep in thought.

THE HURT OF
YOCHANA

"Are you thinking about the diary Jamie?"

"Yes, I think we did the right thing not telling Jane. She seems stable and happy, I'm so pleased we never shared what we know."

"Maybe now we can move on. I was surprised when she said she had decided not to do Caribbean Law but to do European History. Wonder what her thinking was for that?"

"Well I am not sure what job she will get if she gets her degree Millie."

"She will have a plan she is Joan's girl and her Mum knew exactly where she was going in life."

"Yeah, guess you are right. Let's pick up a take-away when we get back home and a nice bottle of red. It might help me come to terms with Jane growing up

THE HURT OF
YOCHANA

Millie." Millie smiled Jamie was such a
kind man and he missed Liam every day
since he died and now Jane going away to
University she knew how he was feeling.

Jane meanwhile was now settled in. She
was sharing with three other girls in Halls
of Residence. Bambi Barratt, Sally
Cummings and Jenny Makepeace. All the
girls had different traits. Bambi was untidy
but very kind hearted, Sally was stunning
looking but a bit dippy and she was
blonde!! Jenny Makepeace was the mother
hen, very sensible, always tidying up and
making sure that there was food and milk
in the halls.

There were four bedrooms, a small
kitchen and a sitting room and a shared
bathroom. Jane had the double bedroom as
she drew bedroom one. Bambi had
bedroom two which was a good job as her

attention to tidiness would have driven
anyone to distraction. Sally Cummings
bedroom three and Jenny Makepeace
bedroom four. The girls all got on well.
They would have to learn to live with each
other's idiosyncrasies.

Jamie and Millie visited every month or
sometimes six week intervals. Jane didn't
mind but sometimes it interfered with
what her and her friends had planned that
weekend. So she was quite pleased when
Millie phoned to say they couldn't make it
this weekend due to Jamie playing in some
golf tournament. So, if it was ok they
would come up the following weekend.

Jane felt a bit guilty feeling pleased she
could now go out with her mates.

THE HURT OF
YOCHANA

"So you are coming tonight then Jane?"
"Yeah looks like Uncle Jamie and Aunty Millie aren't up until next weekend now."
"Ok so what are you wearing for the fancy dress ball at Muckers in town?"
"I am going to go as Snow White. What about you three?"

"Well I am going as a Banana Brilliant Bambi. What about you Sally?"

"I'm going as Miss Haversham out of Great Expectations."

"Blimey makes my banana idea seem naff." Sally and Bambi laughed.

"What about you Jenny I thought I would go as Mary Poppins." They all laughed.

"What's so funny?"

"Because you are flippin' Mary Poppins," Bambi said.

THE HURT OF
YOCHANA

The girls got ready and headed for Muckers. Muckers was a student type pub with a dance floor, it was quite big, but had possibly seen better days. But the drinks were very cheap so the students used it. There was an array of costumes in display, Charlie Chaplin, Marilyn Monroe. Adolf Hitler and Winston Churchill were actually deep in conversation.

The night was quite boozy with Jenny keeping an eye on everyone, just pretending to drink she would be worried until she got all the girls back safe.

"Hey Snow White fancy shaking your bootee for me?" asked the tall dark handsome man dressed as Clark Gable out of Gone with the Wind.

"Why not." The record playing was Bananarama 'Robert De Niro'

THE HURT OF
YOCHANA

"It's Bananarama Bambi," Sally shouted. "Come on let's boogie."

Eventually with Jenny's stewardship they all got home safe and sound.

"I am whacked girls. I'm off to bed. Is Clark going to be in touch?"

"I don't know. He gave me his mobile number he was quite dashing Jane," said Jenny.

Jane left them talking about the night and climbed into bed. This was to be the night when her whole life would change and her journey would begin.

Jane was soon asleep and dreaming. A voice kept whispering, "They need to pay, they need to pay," and in her dream she could see a girl of sixteen or eighteen she thought. She had a brown headscarf and was dressed in rags but her beauty shone like a beacon. Jane woke up with a start."

THE HURT OF
YOCHANA

"Blimey I'm not drinking Gin again," she thought. "What a horrible dream." She went into the kitchen to get a glass of water. The girls had gone to bed. You could see where Bambi had been sitting by the mess round the chair. It was 6.10 am so Jane guessed she had been asleep about six hours. Not feeling tired and with the dream quite vivid she entered the date in her diary and wrote.

"September 24th 2016. Had a great night at the fancy dress ball with my room mates Bambi. Sally and Jenny probably had too much Gin to drink. I had horrible dream. Pretty girl dressed in rags kept whispering They Must Pay, They Must Pay. Avoid the Gin me thinks."

It was 10.00am when the Sally appeared. "Blimey is that the time? Got a lecture at 11.00am. I'd best get going. Jane, you ok? Good night last night." Jane didn't mention the dream.

"Yeah enjoyed it Sally. Do you want a slice of toast before you go?"

"No best get over but thanks Jane." Jane had a lecture at 1.00pm so she went back to her room. Somehow the little pot vase with the plastic rose had blown over and was lying at the foot of the bed, so she picked it up and put it back on the dressing table and made her bed. She was just about to leave when her mobile rang.

"Aunty Millie here." Millie always said that. She didn't realise that Jane had caller identification on her phone or maybe it was just habit on Millie's part.

"How are you? Did you go out with your friends?"

THE HURT OF YOCHANA

"Yes Aunty Millie. I had a great time. Liverpool is so vibrant, it feels a lot safer than London."

"The reason I am phoning, well two things actually. Uncle Jamie said I had to check you were ok but that's Uncle Jamie fussing. The second thing was I saw Marty Haynes in Pizza Hut Saturday and he asked after you. Were you close?"

"Oh, no Aunty Millie," Jane replied in a distasteful manner, "he isn't my type." Millie laughed, "You kids."

"Aunty Millie I am going to have to go, my lecturer is putting on this special class today, as a one off with it being Sunday, and I'd best not be late. Love to you both."

"Take care Jane," and Millie hung up. Jane headed for the lecture. It was entitled 'Is it possible mankind could have done this?'. Jane was intrigued. The lecturer, a

THE HURT OF
YOCHANA

Mr Monroe Skipton, was a tall man dressed in a sports jacket with leather arm pads. He had three pens in the top breast pocket, a pair of unkempt blue trousers and for some reason he wore training shoes which also looked like they were ready for the bin. He looked a studious man, middle fifties, grey hair and he wore round John Lennon glasses which perched precariously on the end of his nose.

"Thank you for coming. A better turn out than I expected from first year students after a Saturday night on the lash." Everyone laughed, Jane and five others that had bothered to turn up.

"Ok let's get down to it. I want to discuss the Holocaust and why people say it didn't happen? So, views please. Yes Mark?"

THE HURT OF YOCHANA

"Well I consider the rationale to be two things. It's a way of people blocking such atrocities from their mind and it also helps the fascist movement gain support."

"Jane?"

"I disagree. People of our generation can't remember the war and the evil done on all sides so it's used as a propaganda tool to keep young people in line by making them think there is a big bad wolf out there if we step out of line."

"Two very interesting takes on the subject. Let's try understanding some reported facts." Mr Skipton turned to the board and started to write. He wasn't what Jane would call a Trendy-Wendy by using power points or overhead projectors and she liked that.

"It is thought by the media that Britain started the first concentration camps during the Boer War. This actually is a misinformed fact. The first concentration camps were in Cuba set up by the Spanish to imprison belligerent villagers in 1896-7, this was called the Reconcentrado Policy. The British did indeed set up what would become known as concentration camps during the Boer War but what we have to remember is these were not death camps. Would not Egypt have had a concentration of slaves in one place when they built the pyramids?"

"What I am getting at is the need to dissect what the British and the Spanish classed as a concentration camp against what the Nazis turned them into. All the time during the 1930's the Minister for Propaganda Josef Goebbels, had postcards printed showing the grim conditions in the concentration camps used by the British.

THE HURT OF
YOCHANA

There was also a film made called OM Paul. So we can conclude that even during the early thirties they had a spin doctor who was trying to convince first the German people, and then the world that the British were the bad guys not the Nazis."

The lecture carried on down the same vein for another two hours. Jane felt enlightened and thought how much she was going to enjoy learning for her degree. She called Millie on the way back to the Halls of residence. Millie could hear the excitement in Jane's voice and how much she was enjoying it.

"You would not believe the lecture today Millie, I really love this course."

"Pleased you are liking it Jane, you have just missed Uncle Jamie he will be gutted."

THE HURT OF YOCHANA

"No worries Aunty Millie, love to you both, speak next week." Jamie had insisted that they pay Jane's contract on her phone to ensure they could always get in contact with her. He was such a fusspot Millie thought.

Jane got back to her accommodation.

"Hi Jane. How did it go at the lecture?" There was only Jenny in the house which was great. Jenny and Jane were best mates, and all though she thought a lot of the other girls she felt she had more in common with Jenny.

"Jenny, it was soooo good I really enjoyed it. He is brilliant at explaining things without boring you."

"Did many turn up?"

"No only six of us, which is a shame as he had given his time up. Some people are just so rude."

THE HURT OF
YOCHANA

"What are we doing tonight Jane?"

"To be honest I could do with writing some work up."

"I'm glad you said that, I wanted to stop in. I think the other two won't be back until about 10.00pm, anyway they have gone to the Street Festival so they will be hammered."

Jenny made them both a coffee and she had bought some cheesecake.

"Oh Jenny my favourite."

"Yes, I love cheesecake. Have you tried that coffee shop up the road?"

"Which one? I don't know the name but a very old Jewish lady and her son run it."

"Oh Ringo's."

"Is that what they call it?"

"Yeah all the student's call it that because he always tells you about Ringo

THE HURT OF
YOCHANA

Starr and his wife eating cheesecake there."

"Ha ha, I see what you mean now. The lady survived the holocaust you know."

"Really I didn't know that."

"Yes she gave me a plastic rose. I think it's for good luck. She said look after the rose and the rose will look after me."

"That's a bit of an odd thing for her to say. Shall we have a bottle of red?"

"Go on then." The girls sat drinking the red wine, talking and watching Poldark on the telly.

"Oh, he is gorgeous isn't he Jane?"

"Just a bit Jenny." Poldark finished and the bottle of wine was empty when they could hear the other girls outside.

"Look they sound hammered and I have a lecture at nine in the morning, so I'm off to bed."

THE HURT OF
YOCHANA

"Me too Jane, night."

"Yeah good night Jenny."

Jane changed into her pyjamas that Aunty Millie had bought her for going away. She snuggled down under the duvet, she felt contended.

Jane was soon fast asleep and started dreaming. Jane could see herself she was about six years old and she was playing in a garden. Behind Jane was a big house. She could see a man and woman sitting on the porch drinking wine and laughing and pointing to her. Jane broke the stem of the rose she wanted to make perfume from the petals. She pricked herself and started to cry.

"Yochana," the lady shouted, "come here to Mummy let me have a look." Yochana's hand had a bit of blood trickling down it. The lady turned to the man, "Get me a bandage Asher for our little girl." The man was her father. He quickly left and came back and dressed her finger.

"Do you think she will be ok Ruth? I mean she could get poisoning."

"Stop fussing. You are alright aren't you sweetheart? What did you do?" She explained that she was picking rose petals for perfume. Ruth smiled and said, "That is lovely but Jacob the gardener might not think so, eh Asher?" and they both laughed. Jane could not remember much more other than at the end she could hear a voice saying "They have to pay" She didn't know what this meant. Jane woke the next morning with the dream fresh in her head. She stretched and got out of bed. The rose vase had fallen over and was on the floor so she picked it up and put it back on the dresser. She will treasure that rose forever she thought.

Jane managed to grab the last of the Crunchie Nut Cornflakes. The house was a bomb site. Jenny said she wasn't cleaning it up and Jane didn't have time. They both left for lectures. On the way Jane told Jenny about her dream.

"You know why you had that dream don't you?"

"No why?"

"Well you had the lecture yesterday and you told me about Ringo's it will have all gone into your self-consciousness."

"Yes, I never thought about that Jenny."

Jenny dropped off at hall one, "See you tonight Jane. I'll cook tea. My lectures are done at 3.00pm."

THE HURT OF YOCHANA

"Brilliant I love your teas said Jenny. What are we having?"

"Not saying, it's a surprise. Ok see you later alligator." It always made Jane smile at Jenny's little sayings. Jane's lecture was on the British Empire and how it was misunderstood by historians. Mr Kelly was the lecturer everyone said wasn't only a lecturer but a letch. This was Jane's first study class with him. The room could hold about thirty students but there were only eleven there; eight girls and three boys present. Mr Kelly, or Simon, as he liked the students to call him was about five foot ten inches tall. He wore maroon spray-on jeans and a green checked shirt. He was going slightly bald and had a full face beard, the type bald men have to prove they can grow hair somewhere Jane thought.

THE HURT OF
YOCHANA

"Ok everyone, settle down you have seen the title of the lecture. Any ideas what I am talking about?"
A pretty blonde girl put her hand up. Immediately Simon strolled over and stood with his arms folded looking down at the ample girl's chest.

"You are?" he said.

"Kylie sir."

"Please it's Simon. Now then Kylie you explain to the rest of the students your thoughts." Kylie seemed quite naive to Simons purvey stare.

"Well what Simon is saying is the British Empire was misunderstood and that it did more good in the world than bad. It made India the country it is today for example." One of the lads sniggered.

"Do you find the lovely Kylie's explanation funny, Mr?"

THE HURT OF
YOCHANA

"Duggan Sir, Chris Duggan."

"So what is amusing you then Duggan?"

"You Sir."

"Oh, so I am funny am I?"

"Well it is unusual to walk round with your zip undone Sir."

Simon didn't know where to put his face but at least it stopped the letching and the lecture carried on. It was quite boring not like the previous lecture but Jane supposed they would not all be great. They finished at 2.50pm and Simon thanked them. Jane left and she called at the Tesco Extra on the way back to buy pasta, mince and tomato puree to make spaghetti bolognaise for the girls. She knew she would pass Ringo's coffee shop so she called in to treat the girls to the Jewish cheesecake.

"Hello, lovely to see you again. I said to my mother I wonder if we will see you again. I am so sorry I never introduced myself to you my name is Robert Klinck. Here let me get you a coffee on the house. Do you mind if I join you, it's been a little slow today?"

"Well thank you Robert that is very nice of you." Robert joined her at the table.

"Were you born in Liverpool Robert?"

"Yes, my mother had me quite late in life. She was thirty eight when I arrived in June 1961. We lived here above the coffee shop. My dad was an American called Walter Klinck. He settled here in Liverpool after the war. What about you?"

"Well my name is Jane Egan. My father was born in Liverpool. I am from a mixed race family hence the olive coloured skin. I was born in London and I am studying European History at Liverpool Hope University. So Robert tell me a bit more about your mum you said she survived the holocaust?"

"Yes, she doesn't talk about it. All I know was her father was a solicitor and she was from a wealthy family in Poland before the outbreak of war. That's pretty much all I know to be honest, she gets very upset if I try to question her. One day two German tourists came into the coffee shop, I am going back twenty or more years ago, my mother would have been in her mid seventies, but she refused to serve them. It was quite embarrassing to be honest but she must have had her reason I guess, with what she went through."

"Oh blimey is that the time Robert. Can you cut me four slices of the Jewish cheesecake? I am supposed to be cooking for my room mates tonight." Robert went in the back and his mother came out with the cheesecake. She handed Jane the box then held her face and kissed her.

"Go in peace my child," she whispered, "they will pay." She turned and went back in the kitchen. Jane was a bit taken back by the words from Maria but tried not to show it to Robert.

"Bye Jane, please call again."

"Yes, bye Robert," and she hurried on back to the Halls of residence.

Luckily for Jane it didn't take her long to knock up the meal. They all sat down to eat and Bambi had brought some bottles of lager.

"This is lovely Jane."

"Thanks Sally."

"Yeah you certainly can cook," the other three said.

"What do you want to do tonight?"

"I have a hot date in town."

THE HURT OF
YOCHANA

"You like the high life don't you Sally?"

"Put it this way Jenny. I am going to make this the best three years of my life."

"Me too Sally."

"Two peas in a pod you two are Bambi."

"What you doing Jane?"

"I need to write up today's lecture."

"That's why I am doing Travel and tourism, its easy Jane."

"I know Bambi but I really want a degree in European History. I intend to do another course and get a couple of languages after."

"Well I bloody don't. I will do this course and hopefully pick myself up doctor, settle down and he can keep me," and she laughed. Jenny wasn't saying much and Jane wondered if she found Sally and Bambi to not be her type.

THE HURT OF
YOCHANA

"Ok time for the treat."

"What is it Jane?"

"Jewish cheesecake."

"From Ringo's?"

"Yes."

"Oh can't wait."

With everyone fed and watered and Jenny cleared the table the other two girls went off to get changed. Bambi had decided to go into town and share a taxi with Sally. Jenny said she was going to Skype her mother so Jane went to her room and started to write up her notes.

It was 10.20pm when she finished so she nipped and got a glass of water. Jenny was still in her room so she knocked.

"Night Jenny."

"Yes night Jane sleep well."

Jane cuddled under her duvet with Sydney the squirrel. Her dad had bought it

THE HURT OF YOCHANA

for her from a weekend away he and her mum had in York. Sydney looked his age but it was a comfort for Jane and it reminded her of her mum and dad who she missed terribly.

Jane was soon asleep. She dreamt she was about sixteen now and it was 1939 when the Germans had invaded Poland. Her father who was a great horseman as well as a doctor went off to fight the Germans. She had been out with my friends and came back and her mother was in the drawing room. She was crying.

"What is a matter mama?" Yochana cried.

"You know your father has been gone for three weeks now to fight the Germans, but on the radio it says all is lost. They have far better equipment than us."

THE HURT OF
YOCHANA

"Mama it will be fine, other countries will help us." Yochana looked round the house at all the nice things and knew this was not going to last. They had just gone to bed when there was a loud banging on the door. Kristen, the servant girl, went to open the door. There was a loud bang as they shot her then trampled on her coming through the house. They grabbed Yochana by her long dark hair and she squealed. One of the men hit her with the butt of his gun. They were all dragged from the house and put into an army truck with a beige cover over the back. Jane could smell the stench in the lorry. They had beaten one old lady so bad she had died and people were crushed on top of her. Children were screaming and women were crying. There were no men in the truck. Jane tried to get close to Mama but they pushed her onto another truck. The guards were laughing as they repeatedly beat a pregnant woman. Next to the truck one turned to the other,

"Schmutzige Ungeziefer." Yochana had been taught German as a language and she translated what the guard said, "Dirty Vermin" They had no respect for age or circumstance as they threw the pregnant women in the truck. She looked at Jane who could see the pain in her eyes. As they set off Jane could see Mamma's truck. It was three trucks away but wasn't going in the same direction as Jane's. They travelled for over seven hours with no water and nothing to eat. They eventually arrived, the town sign said 'Deblun'. There was a very high wall made of barbed wire all around the town. They were pulled off the truck and were thrown on the pavements and the road.

THE HURT OF
YOCHANA

Yochana was one of the lucky ones
because she was young and fit. She looked
for Mama but she hadn't arrived yet and
Yochana was unsure if they were bringing
her there. They were made to stand in line
and an SS officer in leather boots walked
along the line of about three hundred
women of all ages and size. The lady next
to Yochana was a big Jewish woman. One
of the guards poked her then turned to the
SS man and said "Dieses Fett wird man
gut Brennen." Yochana was horrified as
he laughed and they pulled her out and
marched her away. Their words were,
"This fat one will burn well." Jane had not
got a clue what he was talking about but
was scared.

Suddenly Jane woke.

"Do you want any breakfast? It almost
8:45am," Jenny said.

THE HURT OF
YOCHANA

"Oh gosh, sorry I was in a deep sleep."

"We know, we could hear you mumbling in the kitchen."

"Sorry Bambi. What was I saying?"

"I haven't got a clue you shouted something, I think it was in German," and she laughed. Jane felt embarrassed. Jenny had done everyone bacon sandwiches. Bambi and Sally left for lectures and Jane helped Jenny tidy up because they didn't need to be at lecturers until mid-day.

"Are you ok Jane?"

"Yes, fine why?"

"Have you been dreaming again?" Jane knew she could confide in Jenny.

"Well to be honest, yes. I dreamt again last night."

"From the noise you were making it didn't sound like a dream, more like a nightmare." Jane didn't feel she could tell

THE HURT OF YOCHANA

Jenny the full extent of the dreams so she made something up.

They finished cleaning up and Jenny went to sort her stuff out for her lecture so Jane did the same. Because of the rush getting up she hadn't noticed the plastic rose was on the floor with the little glass vase. Damn she thought I must have knocked it over in my rush getting up this morning. Jane placed the rose back in the glass vase and placed it back on the dressing table.

Jenny said goodbye to Jane because her lecture was on another campus. She wandered down the carefully manicured gardens towards her lecture hall. For some reason she decided to phone Millie.

"Aunty Millie?"

"Jane, are you ok?"

THE HURT OF
YOCHANA

"Yes I'm fine I think. I might come and stay with you for the weekend, if that's ok Aunty Millie."

"Of course it's ok. We would love to spend some time with you. Uncle Jamie will be that chuffed."

"Look Aunty Millie I will have to go, I'm at my lecture. I will see you at St Pancras Saturday morning, should be there at 11.10am."

"Ok sweetheart we will be there for you."

Jane arrived at the lecture on Oswald Moseley and Diana Mitford. During the lecture Jane found her mind wandering to her dreams. She was jolted out of her dreams when a student was asked if the atrocities they read about today were actually true. Jane realised the lecturer was trying to evoke debate. It was the answer he gave that troubled Jane.

"I believe there are many views on this, Sir. I also realise that my answer to you may cause consternation within the group but I do not believe the so-called death camps ever existed. We, the British, did far worse things."

If this student had decided to get the debate going it certainly did. The theme of the lecture, Moseley and Mitford, never surfaced in the two and half hours the lecture lasted. As he left the lecture the student who caused the furore followed Jane out.

"Hi, I'm Matt Babington." Jane was a bit taken back by his introduction but shook his outstretched hand anyway.

"I'm Jane Egan."

THE HURT OF
YOCHANA

"I saw you last Sunday in the lecture wasn't he good?"

"Yes, I enjoyed it."

"Do you fancy a coffee Jane?" Jane hesitated for a minute, and then thought what the hell so they headed down to a Starbucks on Wilton Street.

"What would you like to drink Jane?"

"Just an Americano will be fine thank you." Jane studied Matt while he was ordering the coffees. He was about six feet tall with blonde hair and blue eyes. His dress sense was a bit random. He wore beige coloured corduroy trousers and had a brown turtle neck jumper which he complemented with a blue scarf and some retro Adidas training shoes. Matt was quite a good looking man and Jane thought they must be about the same age.

THE HURT OF
YOCHANA

He wandered back with the coffees and placed two rocky road cakes on the table.

"You looked like you needed feeding up Jane, "and he laughed.

"You must be joking," she replied.

"So, are you doing the same course as me, European History?"

"No, I am doing a degree on Politics and World leaders through history. So last Sunday I had free time so fancied the lecture because I know the lecturer is very good. But today my course overlapped because of the Fascist Oswald Moseley, not that we discussed him after I stirred the hornet's nest," and Matt laughed.

"You don't honestly believe what you said, do you Matt?"

"Look I must be truthful with you. I am not sure that all of what they say happened, there was an awful lot of propaganda on both sides."

"So, what do you intend to do with your degree Matt?"

"Hoping to go into politics. What about you?"

"Not sure, if I am honest I really don't know why I went for European History, it was just an idea that came into my head."

"Bit random that Jane," and Matt laughed. Jane thought what a lovely smile Matt had. After a lot of getting to know each other Jane said she needed to get back as Bambi was cooking.

"Ok Jane, would you like to go out one night into town, perhaps this Saturday?"

"Sorry Matt, I am going home this weekend." Damn she thought. As much as she wanted to see Millie and Jamie she quite fancied a night in Liverpool with the handsome Matt.

"Oh ok, I am going to see a group on Tuesday night at the Cavern. They are called Wiki Rebels, they play Punk and a bit of Jam, if you fancy it?" Thank goodness for that Jane thought.

"Yes, that would be nice," she said coyly.

"Ok I will meet you at 8.00pm at yours. Give me your address, and then we can get the bus into town." Jane hurriedly wrote down her address and thanked Matt for the coffee and headed back.

"Hi everyone."

"Come on Jane, you are late," they said. They were all sitting at the table with Bambi in the kitchen.

"Sorry, got talking."

THE HURT OF YOCHANA

"Was it male?" said Sally? Jane blushed as she took her coat off.

"Well actually it was, and I am seeing him next Tuesday."

"Good on yer girl, is he good looking?"

"Well I think so, but then I am biased." Dinner was served. Bambi had made a vegetable bake with bacon which all the girls laughed about.

"Did anybody get any mayonnaise?"

"You and mayonnaise, Sally."

"I know I love it. Mum has heaps at home. I have it on my Christmas dinner." Sally had bought some cans and a bottle of wine and Jenny had got a Bakewell Tart and cream.

"I thought we could have the pudding while we watch the latest Bridget Jones movie."

"Where did you get that from?"

THE HURT OF
YOCHANA

"One of the lads on my course made a pirate copy."

The girls settled down. Having consumed the wine Jane felt a bit bad she hadn't bought anything, and the lager was going pretty fast.

"Pause the film and I will nip down to the off-licence and get some more cans."

"Great, ok Jane." Jenny paused the film and Jane nipped out. On the way to the off-licence she was approached by two lads wearing hoodies.

"What are you doing out here on your own?" Jane just kept walking.

"Hey bitch," one of them shouted. "I am talking to you." Jane's heart was pounding as she arrived at the off-licence. She pulled out her phone to phone the other girls but her phone battery was flat. She got the lagers and poked her head out of the door looking both ways. The boys appeared to have gone so she set off. Jane got about a hundred metres from the halls of residence when she saw something flicker she stopped in her tracks it was a knife blade.

"Now then bitch, I have your attention." Jane knew she had to react and quick, so she spun round and hit the man holding the knife straight in the face and he fell down. She also kicked the other lad between the legs and he fell onto his knees. With that security came running out and the two lads ran for it.

"Are you alright love?"

"I will be fine, thank you," Jane said.

"Did you not see the posters, those two bastards have attacked three women so far."

"No I didn't."

THE HURT OF
YOCHANA

"Well you certainly handled them well."

"Only out of fear I can assure you," Jane said.

Jane got back to the girls and as usual Jenny was fussing over her mate.

"I knew I should have gone with you. Promise me you won't do that again."

"I won't, I can assure you." With all the drinks and the nibbles gone, the girls decided to call it a night and they headed off to their respective rooms. Jane was still running on adrenalin so she made herself a milky coffee and sat up in bed reading Jane Eyre. She loved the story and had read it before. She loved how the Bronte sister wrote and promised herself she would go to Haworth

Jane nodded off and was back again in Poland in Deblun. She felt alone and scared. Where was Mama? They were herded into the town. Deblun was a miserable place people walking round aimlessly they looked so sad Jane thought. Their clothes were just rags and would not keep them warm during the harsh winter that was coming. A woman who looked about eighty dressed in a long skirt and a filthy blouse with a woollen shawl gestured to Jane that she needed food. A young guard saw her begging and he calmly came over and shot the old lady in front of Jane. Jane dropped to her knees and he kicked her and told her to get up. He said in German, "Schmutzige jüdische Hure," which meant dirty Jewish whore. Jane looked at him with totally disbelief that this young man, who must have only been twenty, could have such hatred in his heart. Jane would see this many times in the future. He stared back at Jane and spat in her face. She swore to herself that he would pay for this one day. Jane's sleep was broken by Jenny her flat mate.

"Jane, are you ok?"

"Sorry, I was dreaming," she said. Jenny sat on the bed, "Is it the same dream?" Jane started to tell Jenny what she had dreamt.

"It sound's incredibly sad, Jane."

"It is Jenny but in some respects I can't wait to go back there, it's a really weird feeling. Listen, don't tell anyone will you? People will think I am a fruitcake or something."

"Don't be daft Jane. You must have been thrashing about in your sleep you knocked the glass vase off the dressing table. That's what made me come in to see if you were alright?"

"Is the rose ok Jenny?"

THE HURT OF
YOCHANA

"Yes fine why?"

"Well this is going to sound ridiculous but the lady at the café, you know Ringo's, she gave me the plastic rose and whispered in my ear. It was a bit strange, she said look after this gift and the gift will look after you. She said never forget and remember I am here for you."

"That's an odd thing to say Jane, I wonder why she said that?"

"Her son told me she had been in a concentration camp during the war and had survived, married and had a son."

"Maybe the course you are doing and with also meeting Maria Klinck that day, just triggered your dreams. You are going to stay with your aunty and uncle today aren't you?"

"Yes."

THE HURT OF
YOCHANA

"Well that will help. I am sure that in a different environment you will probably sleep better."

"Sorry to burden you Jenny."

"Don't be soft, we are mates aren't we?"

"Of course Jenny," and Jane hugged her.

"Well I best get my things together, the train leaves shortly"

"I'll walk to the station with you Jane."

Jane and Jenny arrived at the station. Jane bought her ticket and the train was on time. She waved goodbye to her friend and managed to get a seat. Sitting across from Jane was a stern looking man in a suit and overcoat, which you don't see very often these days she thought. He had a white shirt and his tie had a motif on it. He was reading a book called England for England. Just to be nosey Jane looked the book up on Amazon. The book was about the far right in English politics. With the book also being in a Kindle version she could read the first thirty pages. Jane was horrified when she started reading the book. It was by an author called Graham Kinder who was the self-proclaimed leader of bunch of racist nutcases who believed the Jewish situation during the war was all propaganda put out by the Americans and the British to discredit the Third Reich. Jane could feel her temper surfacing. She laid her iPad down on the table and said, "Excuse me," to the man reading the book.

"Why are you reading such rubbish?" she could not hide her feelings. The man looked at her and said in a dismissive way "Who are you? Look at your skin colour, you are no better than a Rhineland Bastard. You should be in your own country. Hitler's teaching said he had no problem with blacks being in their own country but not in Germany." The bile coming from the man so incensed Jane she lost it and slapped him across the face. The man pulled the emergency chord and the train came to a juddering halt. The guard came running to the carriage. The man looked at the guard and said he had been assaulted. He then pointed to the woman across from them who had seen what Jane had done. The guard called for the Transport police and Jane was taken away. She was allowed one phone call so she called her Uncle Jamie. Jane told Jamie what had happened. Jamie laughed and said he would come and get her as she was at Sheffield police station.

Three and a half hours passed before Jane was released with a caution. The man hadn't pressed charges because the woman witness said Jane had been racial abused. Jamie was laughing as they got in the car.

"You are just like your dad. What got you so annoyed Jane?" Jane proceeded to tell Jamie what had happened. She didn't say anything about the dreams but said she was learning about Germany during the war in her course at University.

Jamie and Jane finally arrived at Jamie and Millie's place. Millie ran over and hugged Jane.

"Oh, I have been so worried about you." Jane went through what had happened on the train.

"Well you did right my love. Obnoxious man."

"Thanks Aunty Millie." All Uncle Jamie could do was laugh.

THE HURT OF
YOCHANA

"I wasn't laughing at your situation sweetheart, just the fact it was something your dad would have done." Jane listened but was miles away. For the first time the dark colouring from her mum's side had become a problem, and she had never had that before.

"Jane, Jane you ok?"

"Sorry Aunty Millie I was miles away."

"Do you want to go out to? Be honest."

"I feel tired out Aunty Millie."

"Well go and get in bed and I will bring you a hot cocoa. Uncle Jamie is golfing in the morning and the sales are on in Oxford Street. Shall we go to them?"

"Yeah that would be great Aunty Millie." Millie let Jane settle down and she brought her cocoa and a homemade Blueberry Muffin then left Jane looking at her phone.

THE HURT OF YOCHANA

"Good night love."

"Goodnight Aunty Millie, love you."

"Love you too darling."

"Do you think Jane is ok Millie?"

"Normally Jamie I would say you are being over protective, but what happened today on the train isn't like Jane one bit."

"I know Millie and that is bothering me."

"Look we are going shopping tomorrow while you are at the golf tournament, so I will try and find out what the problem is."

"Do you think she isn't enjoying University life Millie?"

"Don't be daft, what isn't there to like, all that socialising? Anyway, every-time I have spoken to her she says she is loving the courses. Come on stop panicking Jamie let's have an early night."

THE HURT OF YOCHANA

Jamie and Millie climbed into bed and snuggled up under the massive duvet.

"Millie I know I am going on, but I feel guilty not sharing Liam's diary with Jane. I think I will share it with her this weekend." At this Millie sat up in bed.

"Jamie Trench, don't you even think about doing something stupid like that. Jane is a vulnerable young lady who lost both her parents very quickly. Just think how it will make her feel. We are the only two people she can trust, we are her parents now!"

"I know Millie but what if she finds out we knew all this about her parents and we haven't told her?"

"Let's cross that bridge when we come to it."

"Ok sweetheart and Jamie leaned forward and kissed Millie.

THE HURT OF YOCHANA

Jamie was up and gone by 8.30am and the girls sat and had breakfast before going shopping.

"So how is the University life then Jane?"

"I love it Aunty Millie. I have good flat mates. I think a lot of Jenny, she is lovely, the other two are as well. But they are more party animals than me and Jenny."

"Are you seeing anyone?"

"Well I have met a lad."

"What's his name Jane?"

"Matt Babington."

"Is he on the same course?"

"No, he is doing politics and world leaders, I think he wants to be an MP one day. I am seeing him on Tuesday we are going to see a group at the Cavern."

"What where the Beatles played?"

THE HURT OF
YOCHANA

"To be honest, I'm not sure if it is actually the real Cavern. I know they say it is for the tourists."

"Anything else happened in Liverpool?" Jane certainly wasn't going to mention the dreams which incidentally she didn't have last night. She also thought it best not to mention the two guys who tried to attack her.

Once they were shopping Millie was in her element buying clothes and boots for Jane. Jamie had given Millie five hundred pound to spend on the day. Eventually they were both shopped out and decide to have a coffee and something to eat.

"Aunty Millie, can we go to a little Caribbean café Mum used to take me to? It's only just down here on Slaughter Lane."

"Of course, you can lead the way."

THE HURT OF
YOCHANA

The little café was painted green and yellow. It had six tables inside and six tables outside. They sat inside. A tall Jamaican man came to serve them. He had long dreadlocks half hidden in a beanie hat.

"Hello ladies, my name is Eddie, what can I get you?"

"Two coffees please."

"Milk and sugar?"

"Just milk," they both said.

"Here are the menus ladies," and Eddie handed them two menus that had seen better days.

"Think I only want cake if we are going out tonight Aunty Millie."

"Great minds think alike, me too."

Jane chose a Malibu Bombe with peach ice cream and Millie went for the Tropical Coconut and Mango Cheesecake.

THE HURT OF
YOCHANA

"Thought you would have had the cheesecake Jane."

"Think I have been spoilt with Ringo's Aunty Millie," and she laughed.

It was soon Sunday afternoon so Jamie and Millie took Jane to the station for her train to Liverpool. Jamie was fussing as usual with Millie telling him to stop it. Jane was thinking a weekend was about as much as she could handle, not that she didn't love them both, but Uncle Jamie was always so protective.

On the way into Liverpool station Jane's phone rang. It was Jenny.

"What time do you get into Liverpool? I will meet you and we can go for a drink." Jane knew Jenny was playing the mother hen but she didn't fancy walking back on her own anyway.

"I arrive at 8.10pm Jenny."

THE HURT OF
YOCHANA

"Ok I will be there, the other two are going to Liverpool One but I didn't fancy it. I have a heavy lecture tomorrow."

Jane got off the train and walked out of the station and past Timpson the key cutting shop. There was no sign of Jenny. Jane called Jenny on her mobile. It rang but Jenny didn't answer. Maybe she had forgotten they were meeting for a drink.

"Aagh, well," she thought might as well walk back to the University. As she came out of the station there were blue lights flashing and police and ambulances everywhere.

"What's happened?" she enquired to the young policeman dressed in his bright yellow reflective coat with police emblazoned on the back.

THE HURT OF
YOCHANA

"A young lady has been attacked by two lads dressed in hoodies." Jane felt an icy shiver run down her spine, she was thinking about her confrontation the other night.

"Mind please, let the ambulance boys come through." Two paramedics were carrying a stretcher with a young girl clearly distressed. Jane managed to get a glimpse. For the second time in a few minutes her blood ran cold.

"That's my friend," she shouted. "Jenny, Jenny." The young policeman tried to hold Jane back.

"That's my friend, she was coming to meet me."

"DI Minty, can you take this lady aside and get a statement."

"I want to go with my friend."

THE HURT OF
YOCHANA

"Let me take a short statement and then I will take you to the hospital."

"Is she going to be alright?"

"I don't know, I'm not a doctor but she looks knocked about to be honest."

Jane gave the young policeman Jenny's details and the reason she was near the railway station. The young constable radioed for a police car to take Jane to Liverpool General Hospital. Jane found reception and they said she would be on the fourth floor, Devon Ward. A couple of nurses told Jane that Jenny would be up from X Ray in about an hour and to go and get a coffee from the cafeteria. Jane waited one and a half hours to ensure they had enough time. Back at the ward the nurses directed her to Jenny's bed.

Jenny was semi-conscious when Jane sat at her bedside and held her hand. Jenny

THE HURT OF
YOCHANA

listened to the conversation but drifted in and out of consciousness.

"Jenny, can I look at your phone so that I can call your parents?" Jenny nodded. Jane copied the number to her phone to call Jenny's parents once she was outside the hospital. Eventually Jenny fell asleep and the nurse asked Jane to come back tomorrow.

"What's the prognosis nurse?"

"Well she took a nasty blow to the head and she was kicked in the stomach, but nothing untoward showed up on the scan, so we think she may have no lasting effect. I can't promise that and it would be best to speak with the doctor tomorrow. He does his rounds about 11.00am for Devon ward."

"Ok thank you so much nurse. If she is ok will she be allowed home?"

THE HURT OF
YOCHANA

"Not for me to say but I would have thought so."

Once outside Jane rang Jenny's parents. Jane hadn't realised they were on the first leg of a seventy eight day cruise. She didn't want to ruin their holiday so she told them the bare minimum with a few white lies. Jenny's mum asked Jane to phone her the following day with an update.

"I hope its good news," she thought for everyone's sake. She decided to take a taxi back after what had happened the other night and then Jenny being attacked. It had somewhat spooked her. Back at the Halls the other two girls were out partying which was becoming the normal thing. Jane made herself a drink and a sandwich and sat down to call Jamie and Millie. She hoped Aunty Millie would answer because she knew how Uncle Jamie would react.

"Hello Jane how are you?" Jane took a deep breath, glad that it was Aunty Millie on the line. She explained what had happened to her a few nights earlier and then what had happened to Jenny.

"Listen Jane, I will put money in your account every month for taxis. I don't want you walking about until these people are caught."

"That's good of you Aunty Millie but I will be ok."

"No I insist."

"I know I should not ask you this, but please don't tell Uncle Jamie. You know how he worries about me."

"I won't as long as you use taxis from now on."

THE HURT OF
YOCHANA

"Hello," came a call from the hallway. Jamie appeared, "Who's that?" Jane, she has just rung.

"Is she ok? Here let me have a word. Hello young lady, how are you?"

"I'm fine Uncle Jamie, just thought I would give you a quick call to let you know I got back ok."

"Thank you Jane, you know how I worry about you."

"No need Uncle Jamie honestly." Jane and Jamie made general chit chat for ten minutes then Jane said she had to go so they hung up. Jane went to her room and changed it to her fluffy pyjamas that Aunty Millie had bought her and she snuggled down under the duvet.

It wasn't long before Jane was asleep and the dreams returned. She was back in

THE HURT OF
YOCHANA

Deblun and spent most of the first day
trying to find her Mama but no joy. With
nowhere to sleep she found a place under a
steel fire escape of an old factory and cried
herself to sleep. It was 4.00am when a
German soldier hit me with the butt of his
gun and told me to move. I was so angry.

"Where do I move to? Please tell me,"
she said in a stern voice. This argument
woke some of the other people further
down the alley.

"You bitch," he said in German. "I think
you need a lesson." He grabbed her and
tore her skirt. Yochana was kicking and
biting him. He hit her several times, there
was no doubt he was going to rape her. He
laid her down. She had blood coming from
her mouth and he was laughing calling her
a Jewish nigger. Just as he was about to do
the act, from nowhere a man appeared. He

THE HURT OF YOCHANA

was maybe eighteen years old and hit the German officer across the head with ferocious glancing blow from an iron bar. The soldier fell on Jane covered in blood. He had killed him. Jane tried to push him off her but he was too heavy. Two women and another man came and pulled the soldier off her.

"You bloody fool Mateusz. What were you thinking?"

"I could not see that pig rape this woman."

"Now they will hunt you down."

"They will hunt me down anyway. We are all going to die like lambs to the slaughter." Jane just listened and didn't know what to say other than, "Thank you Mateusz, you saved my dignity and my life."

THE HURT OF YOCHANA

Panic set in. They could hear German soldiers shouting for what we assumed was their colleague, "Severloh where are you Severloh?"

"Quick drag the body down the basement." A lady threw Jane a shawl to cover the blood on her and the other two men made good the area where he was killed.

"Fast now, all pretend to be asleep."

"Hey Heinrich look what we have here, pig scum." They started making a noise and laughing, randomly kick people as they went down the alleyway. All the time Jane's heart was pounding. The soldiers carried on still shouting for their colleague. Once they had moved on Mateusz came over to me to ask if I was ok.

"Thank you so much," I replied

THE HURT OF
YOCHANA

"What is your name?" he asked?

"Yochana."

"That's a pretty name. Don't worry about the body. I can sort that with the resistance, they will take it away." Intrigued, Yochana asked him if he was in the resistance. He said he had been an engineer but had connections with the Polish resistance. He said his uncle was high up and he would be joining him in the morning. Mateusz was about six foot tall with blonde hair and striking blue eyes. He had the most wonderful smile and she felt safe with him.

"Yochana, I won't possibly see you again but you need to keep moving. This is a holding camp for the concentration camps and when they see a face regularly they decide if you live or die, and with you being a darker skinned Jew I am afraid your chances are not good. I have a friend who will look after you in the morning. Go to a street called Wydmaj, at the end of the street you will see a big white house. Go to the house and ask for Ruth she will take care of you but you must do everything she says. Do you understand Yochana?" She nodded and thanked Mateusz again for his kindness.

It felt like Yochana would never see her parents again as she wandered the streets of Deblun at first light. Eventually she found the street and could see the white house that Mateusz had described to her. Luckily the streets were quite deserted. She climbed the wooden steps to the house and knocked on the door. After a few minutes the door opened slightly.

"I have come to see Ruth," she said to the lady who would have been about sixty.

THE HURT OF
YOCHANA

"I am Ruth who are you?" She explained that her name was Yochana and that Mateusz had told her to come there. Quick as a flash Ruth opened the door and pulled Yochana inside.

Jane woke from her dream intrigued and wanting to know more. She wasn't frightened for some reason. She looked straight away and the rose and the vase were both on the dressing table. This was a good sign since after each dream previous the rose had been on the floor when she woke.

Jane showered and changed before calling the hospital. Bambi and Sally had stayed out all night. The hospital told Jane good news. Jenny had recovered and was sat up eating breakfast. The relief Jane felt was enormous. She had a lecture at 11.00am so told the hospital to tell Jenny she would bring some clothes and would be there about 2.00pm.

Jane was going to leave a note for Bambi and Sally but there was little point as hopefully Jenny would be home before they even knew anything had happened. Sitting at the kitchen table with her diary poised and ready to write down her dreams Jane felt a sense of foreboding come over her. She could hear Maria Klinck's voice in her head and the words she spoke, "never forget." What did Maria mean that day when she whispered in her ear, that was she never to forget and how would a plastic rose look after her? Jane was beginning to doubt her sanity when her phone vibrated on the table.

"Hey Jane, its Matt. Are you still ok for tomorrow night?"

THE HURT OF
YOCHANA

"Err yes, I guess so. Jane then proceeded to tell Matt about Jenny and the reason she hesitated was she didn't know what sort of condition Jenny would be in when she brought her home.

"Jane if you want to cancel that's not a problem. I could come around with a bottle of wine and a pizza and sit with you and Jenny if that helps the situation."

"Can I call you later today when I know more Matt?"

"Yes of course, like I said not a problem." What a nice guy Matt seemed Jane thought.

Jane left the house for her lecture which lasted almost two hours, and with a bag of clothes for Jenny she set off for the hospital. Jane was surprised to see Jenny sitting on the bed when she arrived.

"How are you Jen?"

THE HURT OF
YOCHANA

"Yes, I feel fine. I am a bit bruised but other than that ok. The doctor said I can come home so I was hoping you had got me a change of clothes."

"There you go," and Jane handed Jenny the holdall.

"Jane you are a star. The police came back this morning and took a statement but they did admit they had little chance of getting anybody for it. I told them you had been attacked a few days earlier. They didn't seem bothered to be honest Jane, although they did say they would have more of a presence round the University for the next few weeks."

"Think they just tell you what they want you to hear."

"Right let me quickly get changed."
Jane and Jenny thanked the nurses and left to go back to the house.

THE HURT OF
YOCHANA

"Jane I really fancy a coffee and some of that nice cheesecake you got from that Jewish café. Shall we call?" Jane felt a little hesitant but also a little intrigued.

"Yes that would be nice," she replied.

They arrived at the aptly named Ringo's café. The café was quite full with students all enjoying Maria's homemade cheesecake. A new girl served Jane and Jenny.

"Two Americano's and two Jewish cheesecakes please." The young girl smiled although not blessed with great communication skills she seemed a pleasant little thing.

"So, tell me Jane have you had anymore dreams?" Jane told Jenny about the latest dream.

"I think you have a furtive imagination Jane," and she laughed.

THE HURT OF
YOCHANA

"Well thanks Jenny. I have to admit it is a bit weird, it's like I am leading two separate lives. The thing is the dreams are consuming me Jen."

"How do you mean?"

"Well I look forward to going to sleep so that I can find out what happened to Yochana."

"Sooner you than me mate. I have enough living this life without anymore," and she laughed.

"Listen Jen, this lad I met Matt, he said could he come over tonight and sit with us. He said he would bring pizza and a bottle of wine."

"Oh, if he is bringing wine, why not?"

"Do you like him Jane?"

"I think I do Jen. He seems different to other boys I have met. He seems caring and kind."

THE HURT OF
YOCHANA

"Grab that one lass you won't find many like that up here."

The coffee and the cheesecake arrived with Robert, Maria Klinck's son.

"Thought I saw you come in Jane. Lovely to see you and who is this?"

"This is Jenny, my best mate at University."

"Lovely to meet you Jenny. I hope you like my mum's cheesecake, you won't get better anywhere."

"Jane bought some a while ago, so I know how good they are, thank you." Robert carried on serving while the girls devoured the scrumptious cheesecake.

With the coffee drank and the plates of cheesecake now a distant memory they thanked Robert and left for the house. On the way they called at the off licence and bought six cans of lager and a bottle of wine. All set for the visit of Matt tonight. On leaving the off-licence Jane phoned Matt.

"Not a problem Jane. I will be at your flat at 7.00pm if that's ok? Do you want me to pick up a film?" Jane said that would be a good idea and he was to surprise her.

Jenny seemed fine and they didn't bother even telling Bambi and Sally because of the drama it would cause. 7.00pm and the doorbell rang. Bambi answered it.

"Come in gorgeous, you must be Matt." Matt had made a real effort in his appearance and looked quite different from when Jane last saw him. Jane introduced him to everyone. Sally was fluttering her eyelashes at him and cursing that her and Bambi had arranged to go out that evening. With just Jane, Jenny and Matt left in the house they settled down with a can of lager and a glass of Chablis each.

"This pizza is very good Matt. Where did you get it from?"

"Just from the local pizza shop down the road. You turn left when you leave your house."

"We never go left, do we Jen?"

"Well there isn't that much down there but a pub, a butcher and this pizza shop. Seems popular though."

"So, go on then what film did you get?"

"It's called Travail. It's about two gypsy families that hate each other. I won't tell you anymore or it will ruin it."

"Who's in it Matt?"

"Brad Pitt and Megan Fox."

THE HURT OF YOCHANA

"Oh brilliant, I love those two," Jenny said. They settled down with Jenny in the armchair and Jane and Matt together on the settee. Things felt right with Matt, Jane thought. Two hours passed and with the film over Matt thanked Jane and Jenny. Jenny made an excuse to go to her room to leave Matt and Jane alone.

"Thank you Jane. I really enjoyed tonight can I see you again?"

"I would love to Matt."

"Ok do you fancy going for a meal on Saturday?"

"That would be great. What time?"

"I will meet you here at 8.00pm I don't want you walking about the city on your own with what's happened to Jenny. Would Jenny go on a blind date with my mate?"

"I could ask. What's his name?"

THE HURT OF
YOCHANA

"Don't laugh but its Simon Canndo."

"Why would I laugh?"

"Every time we introduce him to somebody we say if I can't do it, Simon Canndo." Jane laughed, "Sorry being a bit thick there Matt."

"Jenny, do you fancy a blind date on Saturday night with Matt's mate?"

"What on my own?"

"No, we are all going for a meal."

"If he is good looking Matt, it would be a pleasure," and Jenny laughed.

"Don't think you will be disappointed Jenny."

"Great see you Saturday then." Matt kissed Jane goodnight and left the house. Jane clapped her hands, "Isn't he gorgeous Jenny?"

"He is rather nice, hope his mate is the same."

THE HURT OF
YOCHANA

"He is such a gentleman as well."

"Best get to bed got double lectures tomorrow."

"Ok Jane good night and thanks for a nice evening." Jane changed into her pyjamas and before she went to sleep she texted Aunty Millie to say everything was good, that Jenny was home and she had her first date with a delightful boy, but to break it to Uncle Jamie carefully, and with that she put a smiley face and ended the text.

Jane snuggled down under her big heavy duvet and was soon asleep and back in the world of Yochana.

Ruth's house was very big and clearly she had been a lady of means before all this terrible trouble. She took Yochana upstairs and told her that when German officers came she was to hide behind this secret panel and never, and she really emphasised the **never**, make a sound or they would take her away and she would be shot for harbouring Jews. She said a bell would sound when she went to the door and that was Yochana's warning to hide. She told Yochana that the German officers came at all times of the day and night, so at all times she had to be vigilant. When Yochana asked why they came she said it was not her business and think herself lucky that she hadn't been taken away yet.

Yochana had been at Ruth's house for almost six weeks and the three other Jewish women never spoke, everyone was frightened. Ruth appeared to have parties. Yochana thought she could hear the clinking of glasses and the laughing the smell of cigars filled the house. Ruth gave updates about how the war was going. She was confident it would be over soon. It was December 25th Christmas day 1941 when the penny dropped on what Ruth was doing. Yochana listened in horror as her hiding place was through a secret passage hidden in the big oak wardrobe. Yochana had fallen asleep on the bed but luckily she heard the German soldier talking on his way to the bedroom with a lady. This was a whore house. Yochana felt sick. She could hear the fumblings of the German soldier and the Polish woman pretending to be amazed at him. It was sickening. Yochana had not eaten for almost twenty fours so was glad when the last of the soldiers had left. Ruth came and got her. She could see Yochana had been crying.

THE HURT OF
YOCHANA

"My dear, I have brought you chicken legs. It is Christmas Day. Why are you so upset?" Yochana wasn't sure if she should say but it all came out on a rollercoaster of emotion. Ruth put her arm round her like a mother then she began to cry.

"Yochana, it may be better if I give you a contact and you leave the house. If you were to get upset with what is happening and they heard you, we would be sent away. So we can survive I will give you an address of the Polish Resistance. They will help you. I am sorry Yochana but I have to think of everybody. Now eat your chicken legs, because you have a five mile walk ahead of you and it's snowing out there." Yochana didn't know what to say. Ruth was possibly right, she had felt sick to the pit of my stomach with what everyone was doing just to survive.

THE HURT OF
YOCHANA

It was 11.00pm when Yochana thanked
Ruth and left for the meeting with a man
called Raitis. Ruth had chosen the time to
leave as she said the soldiers would be
indoors keeping warm. As she set off on
the five mile walk to her new destiny the
snow was falling. It was very cold and she
felt chilled, but somehow with it being
Christmas Day she felt a renewed hope
that maybe very soon this dreadful
nightmare would be over. After about
three and a half miles two men and a
woman were sitting in the street. They
were Polish Jews like Yochana. They
offered her soup and bread and a little
vodka which she tried to sip but they
insisted she swallowed the whole glass. It
felt awful. The lady's name was Kristina
and she asked Yochana where she was

going on Christmas night and why was she not with her family?

Suddenly my alarm clock rang and Jane was out of her dream. She lay in the bed trying to understand all this. She was even beginning to worry about Yochana. "Am I going mad?" she thought. She dressed for her lecturers and made her way into the kitchen. Bambi and Sally were laughing. "Ok what's the big joke?"

"Nothing Jane, it's just the noises you make are incredible." Jane could feel herself colouring up, "What do you mean?"

"Well you like shout, and then mumble and were you sick last night, must have been some evening."

"What do you mean sick?"

"We could hear you vomiting?" Jane felt a cold shiver run down her back.

THE HURT OF
YOCHANA

Yochana had felt physically sick listening to the German soldier and the woman in the bedroom. This was getting serious Jane thought. The girls stopped taking the mickey, they could see Jane was upset.

"Look we are sorry Jane. We didn't mean to upset you."

"It's ok just had a nightmare, that's all," and Jane brushed it off. Bambi and Sally left before Jane. Jenny had been listening to the conversation and came out of her room.

"Is it the dreams again Jane?" Jane looked at Jenny and broke into tears.

"I don't know what to do Jenny. What does this all mean?"

"Do you think you should speak with your Aunty and Uncle?"

THE HURT OF
YOCHANA

"I will probably speak with Aunty Millie. Not sure I could handle Uncle Jamie fussing Jenny."

"Look I am away a week on Friday, so they could stay here if you want."

"That is so kind of you Jenny. I will call them on the way to the lecture. How are you feeling?"

"A bit sore but getting there. Not bothering with my lectures until I get back from seeing my friend in Stoke." Jane left and as she walked towards the University she called Millie.

"Aunty Millie"

"Hello sweetheart, how are you?"

"I'm ok. I am ringing to see if you and Uncle Jamie want to come and stay with me a week on Saturday. My friend is going away then and she said you can use her room."

THE HURT OF
YOCHANA

"Just let me check love." The call went quiet while Millie checked the calendar.

"I would love to, but Uncle Jamie is on a stag weekend in Prague with a gang from the golf club."

"Well you come, it would be nice to have some girlie time Aunty Millie."

"Ok sweetheart, I will put it on the calendar and look forward to it." Millie came off the phone and thought she knew Jane well enough to realise something was amiss. What if she is pregnant or doesn't want to carry on with her course. She rang Jamie and told him her plan and he was quick to ask if Jane was ok. Millie shrugged it off. She knew how Jamie would worry and would want to cancel the stag weekend. Millie felt Jamie had not really enjoyed himself since the death of Liam and she knew he missed him daily.

THE HURT OF
YOCHANA

Jane's lecture was on Marie Antoinette, the last queen of France and her influence on the French people. It was a well-attended lecture. Prunella Simpson was quite young and she made the lecture interesting allowing freedom of expression from the students. Jane wanted to know why she attempted to flee in June 1793, when it was clear the chance of her getting away was virtually nil.

"Well," said Prunella, "I would imagine she knew the revolution was the end for her and although she possibly didn't realise they would kill her. The thought of languishing in a dirty smelly jail for eternity made her do what we as humans do. We react." While Prunella was talking Jane got a flashback to her dreams and Yochana would eventually fight back and react she thought. Prunella was still talking when Jane came out of her daze.

"Does that answer your question?"

"Yes, thank you," said Jane.

"Ok anymore questions? Yes, the man in the brown shirt."

"Did Maria Antoinette actually say 'let them eat cake' when she was told the peasants were hungry and revolting?"

"As you know, this is a very famous quote and it is believed when she was told in 1798 that the peasants had no bread she declared "Qu'ils mangent de la brioche" Which means for all you French students "Let Them Eat Cake." This single inhumane quote didn't endear Maria Antoinette to the people and she became a hated figure. She was already disliked because of her Austrian heritage but this somewhat put the icing on the cake as they say. Although history tells us that this quote had been used before in other countries prior to Antoinette's famous quote, so she possibly borrowed it anyway. The peasants had their revenge when she was taken to the guillotine on 16th October 1793 to hideous scream of laughter from her adversaries."

The lecture carried on for a further fifty five minutes. Jane had enjoyed the lecture and spoke with Prunella when it was over.

"Thank you Jane, it's very nice of you to say you enjoyed my lecture. Have you anymore today?"

"Yes Mr Brigden's lecture on Dig for Victory."

"Oh ok well good luck with that one Jane. See you at my next lecture." They parted and Jane grabbed a coffee in the

THE HURT OF
YOCHANA

student room and sorted her books out for
the next lecture at 2.30pm. As Jane made
her way down the halls she heard a voice

"Jane, Jane" she turned around. It was
Matt.

"Oh hi, where are you off to?"

"Two hour lecture on Tony Benn. What
about you?"

"Mine is Dig for Victory". Sounds
better than yours though and she laughed.

"Are we still on for Saturday night? Is
Jenny coming I have lined up Simon."

"Yeah she seems up for it."

"Ok well I will meet you at yours.
Simon is going to meet us at the
restaurant."

"Which one are we going too?"

"My surprise," and he touched his nose
with a nudge, nudge, wink, wink gesture.

THE HURT OF YOCHANA

Very Monty Python. She remembered her Dad loved John Cleese.

Jane had no more dreams and she was feeling a little confused as to why had they stopped. What a crazy feeling she thought. Part of her was aching to know about Yochana but the other part of her wanted a normal life.

"Hey Jenny are you nearly ready? I bet Matt will be here soon. I feel like a schoolgirl on her first date. I wonder what Simon looks like?"

"Matt said he is good looking. Wow Jenny you look fabulous."

"Ah thanks mate you do too." The door bell sounded.

"I'll go," Jane set off down the hall way. She could see Matt's figure through the glass so opened the door.

THE HURT OF
YOCHANA

"Hi," Matt said as he leaned forward and kissed Jane, "Are you both ready?" Jenny came trotting down the hall, "Ready to party handsome?"

Jane could not believe how hyper Jenny was. Matt had a taxi waiting. The girls climbed in the back.

"Troubled Face restaurant mate please. Do you know it?"

"Should do. Quite often take Everton and Liverpool footballers there mate. So what are you celebrating? Not cheap there you know?"

"It's our first real date and Jenny's blind date." Jenny tapped Matt with her handbag, "That sounds awful." They all laughed.

"Right here you are mate, have a nice evening." Matt paid the taxi driver and they walked on a small red carpet that led to the double doors of restaurant. Two doormen opened the door.

"Wow look at this Jane." The restaurant had been an old library in its previous life. There was a man in a dinner suit playing a baby grand piano on a small stage to the right-hand side of the double doors.

"May we take your coats madam?" said the lady.

"We have a table for four under the name of Babington."

"Follow me Mr Babington. Ladies, your friend has already arrived and is seated at your table." They arrived at the table laden with cut glasses and silver knives and forks. Simon got up and greeted them. He pecked both girls on the cheek. Jenny blushed and sat opposite Simon.

THE HURT OF YOCHANA

"This place is tremendous, look at all the Tiffany style glass work everywhere and that beautiful chandelier."

"If you think that is a big chandelier you should see Matt's parent's house." Matt tried to cover up Simon's words but the cat was out of the bag.

"Do your parents live in a big house then Matt?" Jane said. Just at that point the waiter arrived with the menus and the wine list. Jenny's eyes almost popped out of her head.

"Look at that three hundred and fifty pounds for a bottle of red wine. My goodness are we going to drink house water?" and she laughed.

"No I will buy the wine," and Matt said he would buy the meals.

"Flippin' heck Jane, think we have copped for two millionaires." Jane could see Matt wasn't comfortable talking about his wealth but Simon seemed quite happy to.

After the wine was ordered Jenny ordered her meal first.

"Would it be ok to have the Dorset Crab with caviar Matt?"

"Please have whatever you wish."

"Ok I will have that followed by hand dived sea scallops with gratinated cauliflower please."

"Jane?"

"So much lovely food to choose from. I will have lobster with truffle chicken quenelles with pasta followed by farmhouse veal medallions and sweet bread with carrots please."

"Jane that sounds delicious, I will have the same please," said Simon.

THE HURT OF YOCHANA

"Could I have the cookpot of seasonal vegetables and fruit followed by dry aged beef, artichoke and marrow please," said Matt.

"Thank you," said the waiter as he poured their wine and he left.

"So Simon, what course are you doing?"

"Well actually I'm not. I just stay with my good friend Matt."

"Oh well how do you survive then?"

"I have an allowance from my mother and father."

"All sounds quite grand."

"Well I figure you are only young once and that's what I keep telling Matt, why the hell he wants to go into politics when he could be a playboy with all the family wealth is beyond me." Jane could see Jenny was star-struck she could also tell that Matt felt embarrassed.

THE HURT OF YOCHANA

"In Matt's defence Simon, maybe he would like to change the world and leave his mark."

"Well his many times removed relative tried that and look what happened to him."

"Who was that Matt?"

"Anthony Babington, I am sure you know the story Jane."

"So, he was your relative?"

"Yes."

"I don't know the story Matt," said Jenny.

"My ancestor plotted to murder Queen Elizabeth First and to replace her with her sister Mary, known as Mary Queen of Scots. Because of the plot Mary was executed. My ancestor was hung drawn and quartered with his fellow conspirators in fifteen eighty six." The starters arrived but Jenny wanted more of the story.

THE HURT OF
YOCHANA

"I think we did this at school. So do your parents still live where he lived?"

"Very close by, Jenny."

"Wow what an interesting story." Jane could tell that Matt was quite a private person with regard to himself. They all agreed that the meals were excellent,

"Room for dessert anyone?"

"I'm ok Matt," said Jane

"Come on Jenny, sure you could share a dessert with me?"

"I tell you what, why don't we share a dessert also Jane?"

"Good idea Matt." They ordered a lemon and mango coconut tart with raspberry coulis and Simon and Jenny ordered the Coffee and hazelnut truffle with a brandy sauce.

THE HURT OF YOCHANA

With the night over the boys paid the bill and they stood outside waiting to get the girls a taxi back.

"You two not coming?"

"No my buddy Matt has some work to catch up, don't you sonny Jim?" Jane thought it a little strange but let it go. A taxi pulled up and Michael Buble and his wife got out to go to the restaurant.

"That's completed my night Matt, thank you," said Jane.

"Good I will call you tomorrow."

"I'll call you also Jenny," said Simon. The girls waved goodnight as they set off back to reality.

"What did you think of Simon, Jen?"

"To be honest he is a bit outgoing, not my usual type but let's see how it goes."

"I could see you are besotted with Matt."

THE HURT OF
YOCHANA

"Not besotted, but I do like him. What an interesting story about his family I can see why he wants to be a politician now." The girls arrived back at the flat; of course, the other two were out partying; no change there they both thought.

"Do you want a night cap Jane?"

"No I am stuffed, going to get some sleep Jen. Oh, nearly forgot my Aunty Millie will come up next weekend if you don't mind her using your room Jenny."

"Absolutely no problem. Good night Jane, sleep well."

"You too Jen."

Jane climbed into bed and in no time she was back in her dreams she was in a deep sleep and back in Yochana world. Her dream appeared to carry on from the last time, she was sitting with Kristina having just drunk that awful vodka.

THE HURT OF
YOCHANA

"What is to become of us Kristina?"

"I don't know my daughter and son were taken from me. My husband never came back, they took him two weeks earlier."

"Who are the two men?"

"You are safe Yochana, the big one is Aron and the slightly smaller one is Cibor. They have been hiding from the Nazis. Almost all the men and the children have gone from the town and the women will be next. They send them to work camps to aid the German war effort." Yochana realised she had been talking for an hour and needed to get going before the soldiers were back on the streets.

"Thank you for your time Kristina but I really must get on my way."

"I understand you don't want to tell me where you are going but I wish a safe

THE HURT OF YOCHANA

journey and pray we may meet another day in better circumstances." Yochana thanked the two men and she carried on drudging through the cold white snow. The town seemed so eerily quiet. Yochana's feet were aching, the holes in her shoes made her feet so wet. A tear trickled down her cheek. Where was Mama? Would I survive this? She felt so alone and frightened. It was 3.38am when she arrived at the address that Ruth had given her. It looked like it had been a social club of some kind. The place was in darkness and she knocked first on the door then on the windows. Suddenly a man opened the door, he had a gun and he grabbed here and pulled her inside. It was Mateusz.

"We meet again," he said.

"Oh I am so pleased it is you Mateusz."

THE HURT OF
YOCHANA

"You will be safe with us as long as you do everything we tell you. Do not take chances it will cost lives. Carry this and Mateusz thrust a gun in her hand.

"Is it loaded?" she asked.

"It better be Yochana," and he laughed.

"I have made a bed for you, follow me." Mateusz took her to the back of the room and slid the wall to one side which took her to a secret passageway. In there were five men and two girls about Yochana's age. They all nodded to her. They weren't malnourished like the other people she had seen.

The following morning they had eggs for breakfast. Yochana was so hungry and ate like a pig. Mateusz laughed at her.

"Steady Yochana, you won't go hungry here, will she Yitzhak?" Yitzhak was a big man with a rifle slung over his shoulder.

THE HURT OF
YOCHANA

He had a big beard and he didn't speak much but just nodded in reply to Mateusz.

Mateusz asked Yochana to follow him to another room. The room was quite bare other than a table with coffee stains and an overflowing ashtray.

"Please sit down Yochana." She sat down feeling very nervous.

"First of all we all need to know we can trust you Yochana. The Nazis are looking everywhere for us. They will promise people their freedom but understand once they have information on us they will shoot you, there is no freedom for a Jew. Are you clear on that?" She nodded.

"Ok you are safe here. We know when the soldiers are coming to search."

"How do you know Mateusz?"

"I can't tell you but we do. Our sole aim is to try and free as many of our people as

THE HURT OF YOCHANA

possible. We have contacts in Britain who help us. The reality is Yochana that the ghettos are just holding camps, anyone who leaves here via the Nazis will die in the death camps. Not all the Germans are bad men, some are sympathetic to us. That's how we know when the searches are going to take place. For you to stay with us you will have to help in the fight against the Nazis or take your chance on the streets. The reason I asked you to come in here was to give me an answer. Are you with us or do you want to take your chances Yochana?" She didn't hesitate, "I am with you Mateusz."

"Good then we have work to do but first take this." Mateusz handed her a gun. "Be careful it is loaded. Only use it when there is no other option. Remember our aim is to stay underground and try and save these people."

"Jane, are you getting up?" She woke out of the dream. Again the rose and the vase were on the floor.

"Sorry I was in a heavy sleep. What time is it Jenny?"

"It's 2.20pm."

"Blimey I slept well."

"I was going to leave you but I could hear you talking and assumed you were having the dream." Jane looked at Jenny the look was enough.

"Where are Sally and Bambi?"

"They have gone to the party in the park. It sounds quite good, they have twelve tribute bands on."

"Shall we go down then Jen?"

"Can do if you want. Why not it will finish off the weekend. Jane you know you can talk to me anytime about these dreams."

"I know Jenny but it's something I have to work out for myself. Come on let's not be morbid let's go and see the Bootleg Beatles." When the girls arrived at Sefton Park they could hear Gerry and the Pacemakers belting out 'Ferry Cross the Mersey' as they approached the entrance.

"That will be ten pounds each ladies," said the old guy at the make shift kiosk.

"I'll get this Jenny, you buy the hot dogs."

"Enjoy ladies, here don't go in without your program."

"Jen this is quite an impressive line-up. Look next on is The Blondie Tribute."

"Look Jane, a beer tent come on girl let's do this. Two pints of Rosie Malone please."

THE HURT OF
YOCHANA

"It's 9.4% proof ladies."

"That will do nicely thank you." The two pints were very cloudy, with very small bits of apple still evident, a sure sign it was strong Jane thought.

"We don't see much of Bambi and Sally do we?"

"Think they think we are a bit stuffy Jane."

"Really I can party with the best of them and I know you can Jen," and she laughed "Let's have a dance." They danced to most of Blondie's songs then moved onto another stage where a T Rex Tribute band was playing.

"Always thought he was gorgeous Jane, all that dark curly hair." The guy singing was really in character. Everyone was clapping and whistling. Before they knew it the bands were finished. It was 9.30pm

THE HURT OF
YOCHANA

so they grabbed a taxi and headed back.
Once inside Jenny made them both a
coffee.

"I really have got the munchies Jane, do
you want a crumpet while I am doing
myself one?"

"I'm ok Jen to be honest, I feel a bit
squiffy after drinking all afternoon. I am
going to bed." Jane wanted to go to sleep
to get back to Yochana and she didn't
have long to wait as once asleep the dream
started again.

"We are taking a little girl and her father
today. His wife was caught by the Nazis
and he will never see her again. I feel we
owe that little girl a chance with her
father, Yochana."

"How do we do this?"

"We go to the slum where they are. We
don't introduce ourselves, just make like

we are from another town, and the
Germans have put us here. Then tonight
we wake the father and the little girl when
we have a sixteen mile trek to get to one of
our men who will then take them all the
way to Scotland."

"Why do we not just take them in the
day why all the secrecy?"

"Did you not listen to me when I said
we can't trust anyone? The Nazis have
started planting spies everywhere, we just
can't take chances. Come on it's time to
go."

Mateusz knew all the back alleys where
the soldiers would not be. When they
arrived there were two little boys, a
woman and a man and his little girl.
Mateusz said we were man and wife, and
then he started asking loads of questions.
Yochana thought this was to see if anyone

THE HURT OF
YOCHANA

was a German spy. It was just before
midnight when Mateusz woke her.

"Come on," he said. "It's time." He held
the little girl's hand and told her not to be
frightened. The man could not believe his
luck as he and his daughter were given
new identity papers. They set off but it
was snowing again. Mateusz put the little
girl on his shoulders. The poor little mite
had no shoes and it was so cold and harsh.
Yochana's feet felt like blocks of ice
where the snow was coming through the
holes and the splits in the soles. They
passed many small ghettos on the way and
the people looked so ill. Most were
coughing and huddled together trying to
keep warm. What kind of race could do
this to these human beings she thought?
Mateusz said they were about one and a
half miles from handover. From nowhere

THE HURT OF
YOCHANA

two soldiers appeared and her heart ran
cold.

"What have we here Fritz?" one of the
soldiers said. He came right up to Mateusz
and stared him in the face with his evil
eyes. He barked at him "Sie Legte", which
meant put her down. Mateusz obliged but
he could see he was angry. Next, he came
over to Yochana and fondled her. She
couldn't help herself and slapped him hard
across the face. This action caused the
other soldier to pull out his gun. Mateusz
wrestled him onto the snowy ground. The
soldier that had fondled Yochana went for
his gun, so the man they were taking for a
new life attacked this soldier. Mateusz
broke the soldier's neck that he had been
fighting, and then went to help with the
other soldier. Mateusz was too late. The
soldier had his gun and shot the man then

THE HURT OF
YOCHANA

he pointed the gun at Mateusz. Just on instinct Yochana fired the gun that Mateusz had given her and the soldier dropped to his knees.

"Quickly, help me drag the bodies across here." There was a small wooded area and we rolled them down the embankment. The little girl was screaming for her Papa. Mateusz took his scarf off and gagged the poor little girl.

"Come on Yochana, we have to get out of here it will be swarming with soldiers in no time." They hurried the rest of the way without incident and handed over the little girl. Yochana hugged her and kissed her.

"Take care my friend," she said to the man tasked with getting the little girl to safety. He nodded and disappeared in the woods with the little girl. She was still sobbing as she left. The emotion Yochana felt was unbelievable. She had shot a man and said goodbye to a terrified little girl.

"What now Mateusz?"

"Thank you for saving my life Yochana. That was a pretty good shot for your first time." Yochana just smiled, it wasn't something she was proud of.

"We have to take a longer way back Yochana, follow me." They headed into a wooded area where Yochana could hear dogs barking and light being shone everywhere. All she could do was put her faith in Mateusz.

Jane woke from the dream and immediately looked over at the vase and the rose. They were both intact on the dressing table which she took to mean it was good. The clock said 7.30am, so she got up and showered. Nobody else was up so she sat and had a slice of toast and a coffee. Jenny was next up but no sign of Bambi or Sally.

"They will not pass the course," Jane said, "it's just an excuse to come away from home and have a good time."

"What time's your class Jen?"

"Just got one at 10.00am but not doing any this week. Like I said, I will wait until I get back from my mates on Monday."

"What about you?"

"Double again, I am afraid; one at 9.30am and another 1.00pm. Really enjoying it though Jen."

"That's good, I can tell."

"Right I best finish getting ready. See you in a bit Jen. Don't forget I am cooking tonight. I can't imagine those two will be here for it though," and she smiled.

"Ok Jenny thanks."

THE HURT OF
YOCHANA

The two courses that day were on the
Roman Empire and Churchill. Jane arrived
at the Roman Empire class and this
appeared poorly supported. Once the
lecturer started she could see why. He had
such a monotone voice it almost sent her
to sleep. The lecture finished and she
grabbed a salad bowl and water in the
canteen. To her surprise Matt was in there
talking to a pretty girl. He didn't seem
fazed to see her, instead he introduced her
as Laura May Pegg. Laura looked about
twenty four with striking long blonde hair
and blue eyes. She stood up and shook
Jane's hand. Matt introduced Jane as a
friend. Jane felt a little bit miffed. It was
like he didn't want this girl to know who
she was or that he was seeing her. Jane
was about to join them when Matt turned
and said, "I will give you a call in the

week." Jane just said, "ok" and returned to where she had been sitting. She watched as he laughed and joked with her. Jane finished her dinner and left. She was so mad she didn't say goodbye, just went onto the next lecture.

Jane came out of the lecture and phoned Aunty Millie.

"Hello sweetheart," came the voice on the other end. Jane so loved Aunty Millie and didn't know what she would have done without her after losing Mum and Dad.

"Have you been to some lectures today?"

"Yes, the first one was a waste of time," she replied, "but the second one I really enjoyed."

"What was that about Jane?" she asked

THE HURT OF YOCHANA

"The Churchill Years, Aunty Millie. The lecture was very good I thought, with lots of interaction with the lecturer and the students."

"I suppose, like most things, we get on with some people and not others, so it will be the same with your lecturers Jane."

"Guess so, are you still coming up for the weekend?"

"Yes, I am looking forward to it. Uncle Jamie has given me some money to treat you with."

"Is he there Aunty Millie?"

"No sweetheart, he is worrying me a bit though Jane. It seems to be all work at the minute for him. Anyway, enough of that. Shall I meet you at the train station Saturday morning Jane?"

"Yes, what time does your train get in to Lime Street?"

THE HURT OF
YOCHANA

"11.10 am."

"I'll be there, can't wait to see you."

"You too sweetheart take care." With that Jane hung up. Millie thought it odd that Jane kept ringing, not that she wasn't pleased, but just wondered if there was more to it. Just then Jamie came in from work.

"You ok love? Look like you have seen a ghost."

"I was coming back from work and passed Liam's old place and I could have sworn I saw Liam."

"Wishful thinking Jamie."

"Probably."

"While we are on that subject do you think I should take Liam's diaries with me at the weekend and discuss with Jane?"

"Oh I don't know Millie."

"She has the right to know."

THE HURT OF
YOCHANA

"I would like to be there when we tell her."

"Ok look, I will broach the subject this weekend and if she seems interested then I will invite her down and we can show her together."

"Ok that sounds sensible Millie."

Jane was by now back home. Jenny was cooking toad in the hole.

"Where are Bambi and Sally, Jenny? Shall I lay the table for them."

"No, you had better sit down, I have something to tell you."

"What?"

"Bambi came back about a couple of hours ago, and announced that she and Sally were going to live with some bloke in town, and they were packing their courses in."

"Wow, not surprised though are you?"

THE HURT OF
YOCHANA

"No not at all, surprised they have lasted this long to be honest. Can we afford the extra rent?"

"I can Jen, what about you?"

"Yes, think so. It will be better for us mate."

"I agree." With the table laid the enormous toad in the hole was presented by Jenny.

"Wow Jen how do you get the Yorkshire pudding to rise so high?"

"My Grandma taught me. She said to whisk the mix by the back door and that gets loads of air in it."

"This is blooming lovely Jen, thank you."

"So how has your day been Jane?"

"Not particularly good. The first lecture was rubbish, then I called for a sandwich in the canteen and saw Matt with this

THE HURT OF
YOCHANA

pretty girl. So, I went over and he dismissed me like he didn't know me."

"Really, Matt did? I thought he was such a nice guy. Simon called me today I am going out with him tomorrow. I will see what I can find out."

"No don't bother Jen he had his chance. I'll wash up Jen."

"No, I cooked so I will wash up. You do the same when you cook."

"Ok that seems fair. I am going to my room to write up my notes Jen, then going to have an early night."

"Ok mate, see you in the morning." Jane sat at her desk in the bedroom and wrote up her notes. All the time she was thinking about Yochana and how this was consuming her life. It was 11.31pm when she finished so she slipped into bed and was soon fast asleep.

THE HURT OF YOCHANA

Yochana's feet felt very cold. The woods were eerie as Mateusz led her through the thick bramble. Her legs were bleeding but she didn't want to moan as she was sure Mateusz could have gone a lot faster without her. Mateusz held her hand as they tried to run through the snow.

"There is a wide stream running through the woods. If we get through that the dogs will lose the scent." He had no sooner said the words when from nowhere came a big German Shepherd dog. It was snarling as it jumped at Mateusz. They rolled down the banking towards the stream. Yochana slid down after them. She daren't shoot the dog for fear of the soldiers hearing it. Suddenly she heard a whimper and the dog lay dead. Mateusz had pulled the poor animal's legs apart.

THE HURT OF
YOCHANA

"Come on," he said, "don't stand staring at the damn thing." They waded into the stream and across to the banking on the other side. Luckily it appeared that the dog must have broken loose from its handler because they could see the lights heading to the east, which luckily was the opposite direction so they could not pick up the footprints which was the other concern. Yochana could have cried with the pain and the way her body was hurting. Her feet were on fire and bleeding. She was bruised from when she had slid down the banking. They arrived back at the safe house and Mateusz got one of the girls to dress her wounds and they gave her some small boots. They were better than the shoes and the days of worrying how she looked were well gone, it was all about survival now.

THE HURT OF
YOCHANA

"Sleep well Yochana, you did good tonight," said Mateusz. Yochana slept well, and was pleased with his kind words.

Yochana woke the following morning to a small disagreement being played out between Yitzhak and Mateusz.

"Where has Marsha gone Yitzhak?" Marsha was one of the girls in the house.

"She said she would be going to find her mother in Gumpsire."

"She is a bloody idiot, they don't let you out of the ghettos. They will shoot her."

"Let's try and find her before the Germans do." Yochana was limping quite badly but it didn't matter as she set off with Mateusz and Yitzhak to try and find Marsha. The faces on the poor people as they passed them by was heart breaking, they were holding their hands out begging

THE HURT OF
YOCHANA

for food. They had been diving in out of side streets to avoid the soldiers when they could see in the distance Marsha was with a soldier he was shouting at her and she was crying. The next thing he hit her so hard with the butt of his gun her skull smashed open. Yochana almost screamed. The soldier then kicked her in the head and walked away to before lighting a cigarette and laughing with a fellow soldier.

"Come on, there is nothing we can do for her." It was almost three hours before they were safely back at the house.

Jane woke from her dream but the vase and the rose were on the floor and the vase had a crack in it. Jane picked it up carefully and put it back in place on the dressing table with a real feeling of doom. It was 9.30am so it had been a long sleep.

THE HURT OF YOCHANA

Jenny had gone to see a girl she knew from back home but said she would be back for dinner. Jane decided to walk up to Ringo's as she needed the company. When Jane arrived at Ringo's there were no customers. She sat for what seemed like an age then Robert came out. He had been crying.

"You ok Robert?"

"Mum passed away last night." I felt a shiver run down my spine. The dream came flooding back to me.

"I am so sorry Robert. Was it peaceful?"

"No, I am afraid she slipped going to the toilet and cracked her head open and she bled to death. I found her this morning." Jane got up and put her arms round him.

"Here let me make you a coffee, Robert sit down." Jane made two milky coffees. They sat for almost three hours, poor

THE HURT OF YOCHANA

Robert was devastated. He asked Jane if she would go to the funeral with him as he had no friends and his mother didn't. Jane said she would and that she would look in on him the next day. Robert said he was shutting the café for a few days as he could not handle the customers asking where his mum was. Jane agreed that was probably a good idea. Little did she know the true effect his mother's death had on poor Robert?

Jane was cooking tea for herself and Jenny when there was a knock on the door. Two police officers were stood in the doorway.

"Are you Miss Jane Egan?" they asked.

"Yes is this about the attack on me the other week?"

THE HURT OF
YOCHANA

"No I am afraid not, may we step inside?" The officers followed Jane into the living room.

"Please take a seat Jane."

"What's this about?"

"I am sorry to say," the lady officer said, "but we have found a friend of yours this afternoon, Mr Robert Klinck"

"What about Robert?"

"I am afraid he committed suicide. He was found by a delivery man at 4.00pm this afternoon. When was the last time you saw him?"

Jane went through everything they had spoken about and how upset he was about his mother dying but she didn't expect this.

"How did you find me?"

THE HURT OF YOCHANA

"He left a suicide note. Would you like to read it Jane?" The lady officer handed Jane the three page note.

"Dearest Jane,

The day you walked into mine and my dear mum's life was the happiest day of our lives. You see Jane, Mum had been waiting for you to come, she always said you would. That day when you came in the shop with what we thought was your parents. My mother called me into the back she said that is Yochana."

Tears were rolling down Jane's face.
"Are you ok Jane?"
"Yes" and she carried on with the note.

"You see Jane, my mother said she knew you and that you would save her sister one day. I thought these were just ramblings from an old lady but I know this not to be the case. Jane there is a will and there is a box that you need to see. When you have read this note go to Simpson the solicitor in Lime Street. They are expecting you. Thank you my dear sweet Jane but it's time to leave. I am sorry to burden this with you but my mother said you would understand. Mum was right they need to be punished."

At the bottom of the note he had scrawled Robert

Jane sat totally in shock she could not believe what she had read.

"Miss Egan are you ok? We will need to take the note for forensic examination but if there is nothing untoward you may have it back. Do you know if they have any family?"

"In the note there is a mention of a sister," Jane said to the lady police officer.

"Where does she live? This is going to sound crazy I hardly knew Maria and Robert, we probably only met three maybe four times."

"I have to say Miss Egan, I do find this very strange." The lady officer took my details.

"We will be in touch Miss Egan." Jane felt like a criminal as they left. How did she explain any of this, her dreams, meeting Maria and Robert, the suicide note? Jane was just about to phone Aunty Millie when Jenny came home.

"Hey mate, that smells good what are we having?"

"Chilli Con Carne and rice."

THE HURT OF
YOCHANA

"Oh you little beauty, can't wait. I bought a bottle of red home with me."

"I thought you were seeing Simon tonight?"

"No he baled on me."

"Why?"

"He said he had a business meeting."

"Thank goodness for that Jen," and Jane started to cry.

"Hey Jane, come on what's a matter?" She started to tell Jenny about what happened in the dream, then the events that followed and how she felt like she was going crazy. Jenny calmed her down and they sat and had their evening meal. Jenny said that Jane should phone Millie and see if she could come a day earlier and go with her to the solicitor. Jenny was leaving tomorrow to go home to see her friend or she would have gone with Jane.

THE HURT OF YOCHANA

Jenny said she would wash up while Jane rang Aunty Millie. Jane composed herself, cleared her throat, then Aunty Millie answered and she cried.

"Whatever is a matter Jane?

"It so complicated Aunty Millie." Jane just could not control herself, all the emotion came out.

"Can you come tomorrow so I can tell you everything?"

"Yes of course, that shouldn't be a problem. Do you want Uncle Jamie to come as well?"

"No I love him, Aunty Millie, but you know how he worries. Please don't say anything until I have told you everything."

"Will you be ok tonight Jane? I can set off now."

"No, its ok, Jenny is with me."

THE HURT OF
YOCHANA

"Ok, well I should be at the train station for 10.38 am."

"I will be there Aunty Millie." Millie came off the phone thinking, I know boy trouble when I hear it little was she to know the extent of Jane's concerns.

That night Jane didn't have a dream and woke up quite refreshed although still apprehensive with regard to the solicitor's visit and the thought that she had to tell Aunty Millie about her dreams. Jenny had left a note wishing her luck. Jenny had left at 7.30am to get her train. Jane sat with a bowl of Crunchy Nut Cornflakes staring at the wall. Why had she not dreamt last night? Was it now over because Maria was dead? Was the cracked vase a sign? Suddenly realising it was 10.10am she grabbed her coat and hat and set off for the train station. It was manic approaching the station. Commuters were everywhere as some trains had been cancelled because of the weather. Jane was hoping the London train had not experienced any disruptions. Her fears were unfounded as the 10.38am train pulled into platform one and Aunty Millie got out of the carriage. Jane was so pleased to see her and ran up and threw her arms round her. Jane needed a cuddle.

"Hey sweetheart, I'm here now. Come on let's go in that Costa Coffee for a coffee and you can tell me all about it." Millie got the coffees and a white chocolate muffin for each of them. She sat down, "So boy trouble I am guessing?"

"No Aunty Millie not that."

"What then?"

"Remember the old lady at the cheesecake shop and her son Robert?"

THE HURT OF
YOCHANA

"Yes, nice people, and even nicer cheesecake. In fact Uncle Jamie asked me to get him some to take home."

"Well that isn't going to happen. Maria the old lady fell over smashing her head and she is dead. Then her son Robert committed suicide." Millie looked shocked.

"Oh, how sad, but how does this relate to you being so upset?"

"This all started that day we went to the cheesecake café and Maria whispered in my ear and gave me a rose, remember?"

"Yes, I do. I said to your Uncle Jamie it seemed a bit odd."

"She said, 'Never forget what they did' That night I had a dream and I kept hearing those words over and over again. The following day I had a lecture about the holocaust and other things. That night I

THE HURT OF
YOCHANA

dreamt I was a girl called Yochana."
Millie almost choked on a piece of the
Muffin.

"You ok Aunty Millie?"

"Sorry Jane, it went down the wrong
hole carry on." Millie had started to see
that Jane was having the dreams similar to
her father. Jane carried on explaining each
dream in a vivid manner. She also told
Millie she had kept a diary. When she had
told Millie about all the dreams she
explained to her about the suicide note
from Robert. At this point Millie had a
tear trickle down her cheek. This poor girl
was going through the same torment her
father had. How could she hide Liam's
diary anymore from her, or would that
create even more anguish for Jane? What a
dilemma she thought.

THE HURT OF
YOCHANA

"Aunty Millie, the solicitor's is just around the corner."

"Ok, let's finish our drinks and go and see them."

The solicitors was literally two hundred yards around the corner from the station. A well-dressed middle aged lady showed Jane and Millie to Mr. Simpson the assigned solicitor's office. Mr. Simpson was a tall man, Millie thought how he looked a bit like John Cleese.

"Graham Simpson, solicitor of Mrs. Klinck and Robert Klinck. Please be seated." The lady that had shown them to Mr. Simpson's office now arrived with a pot of tea, china cups and a plate of Rich Tea biscuits. She poured the tea then left the room.

"Firstly, if you could introduce your selves and do you have any identification with you? I am sorry to ask this, but I have to be careful if I am going to hand over a deceased person's effects." Jane looked at Millie inquisitively. She wasn't expecting to be given anything, just an explanation. Jane showed Mr. Simpson her passport and Millie luckily had her passport too.

"Ok thank you for that ladies." He got up and walked over the paneled wall where a picture hung. He removed the picture to reveal a safe.

"You couldn't make this up," Millie thought. Simpson returned with a tattered shoebox from the safe.

"Before I go any further, with regard to the will, I can't read the will until the death certificates have been released. This may take a week but I will inform you in writing if you leave your address with my secretary before you leave today." Again

THE HURT OF
YOCHANA

Jane was shocked. Mr. Simpson released the tatty old string which was wrapped round the shoe box. Inside were some pictures and some other personal things.

"I won't go through the contents, Maria Klinck was adamant this was for your eyes only. With that in mind we are done here today ladies. Thank you for your time. I am very sorry for your loss and I bid you good day, but I will be in touch." Jane and Millie left the office and informed the secretary of their address.

"Look Jane, that box meant something to Maria Klinck. I don't know why she singled you out but it all seems like destiny. If you don't want to share the contents, I won't ask."

"Aunty Millie, I need you with me when I start going through this box."

THE HURT OF
YOCHANA

"Ok then, let's go back to your house, make a coffee and look at the contents." Millie felt a sense of déjà vu. She had been thrown something similar with Liam she decided she could not burden Jane with Liam's diary at the minute. They arrived back at the house and Jane placed the old shoebox on the kitchen table while Millie made the coffee.

"Ok are you ready Aunty Millie?"

"I'm ready sweetheart best get it over with." Inside the shoe box there were pictures of two little girls playing, they had blonde hair and pig tails. There were two more pictures which Jane thought may have been Maria's mother and father and grandma and granddad. There was a pair of John Lennon type glasses. Two small teeth in a little tin. Then the most bizarre discovery of them all. A key with a note.

THE HURT OF YOCHANA

The heading on the note was 'Never forget what they did' the note went on to say "Yochana, when you get to read this note I am sorry but your life will be in danger". The Nazis are still out there and when you release the paperwork your work will be done. Once you unlock the safe holding the details you will need a further code which you will find above the gates when you enter Drigden Schlup Concentration Camp. Above the gates there is a wrought iron sign and on it are two numbers at the beginning and two numbers at the end with the verse in between. Take the numbers and they will release the document. If you release the document you are almost certainly signing your death warrant. You will find the safe hidden in a church in Paisley in Scotland. A kind survivor became a vicar and he hid

THE HURT OF
YOCHANA

it until the day Yochana would release this on the world. The safe is behind the picture of St John the Baptist. The church is St Matthew in the village of Grove, three miles out of Paisley. You will need the numbers, that way it is Yochana the chosen one, who will release this information to the world, Good luck my dear your people wait on you.

Maria Chayobbi (Klinck)"

"This is all very weird Aunty Millie. It all ties up with the dreams. I am guessing her sister will make herself known to me in my dreams and that I will see these numbers." It was on the tip of Millie's tongue to explain about her father Liam Egan and his diary and regression, but she was such a child Millie thought.

"Put the box away, it appears nothing happens until you dream about these people and the numbers. So let's go and have some retail therapy sweetheart," Millie said. Once in town Millie worked hard to cheer poor Jane up. They had a full day shopping but Jane was distant, it was as if she was desperate to get back into Yochana's world. Once back at the house Jane said she was tired. Millie decided to stay up and watch a film. Jane kissed her goodnight and headed for bed.

The following morning they were both up about 10.00 am. Millie was desperate to know if Jane had found anymore out during the night. Millie had looked up the name Yochana and its equivalent western name was Jane or Joan. Even Millie was starting to think there was something bigger to all this. Jane's first words to Millie were, "I didn't dream Aunty

Millie," and she could see the disappointment in Jane's eyes.

"Never mind sweetheart, maybe that is a good thing, you are being left alone now." Millie didn't tell Jane about the name or the fact she had found out about St Matthews church in Grove, just outside Paisley. She decided to keep that to herself for now. She didn't want to talk about it, hoping that Jane would then not have any more dreams and this would all go away.

"So what shall we do today Jane?"

"What if we go to the big antiques fair in Sefton Park, I know how you love antiques," said Jane.

"Uncle Jamie is testament to that Jane," and for the first time since Millie arrived Jane laughed.

"Let's get a taxi, can't be bothered with buses. Anyway, we need to spend this money Uncle Jamie gave us Jane." The girls got a taxi to Sefton Park. It was free entry but there was a charity box for the troops so Millie put ten pound in the box. A soldier thanked Millie and smiled at Jane.

"Think you copped there Jane."

"What does that mean?"

"Oh, when I was a young lady like you if my friends said somebody fancied you we called it copping off."

"Weird Aunty Millie, just weird," and she laughed. They wandered in and out of the tents when they came across a beautiful grandfather clock which Millie fell in love with. While Millie haggled with the owner Jane went to look in the tent. At the back was Nazi memorabilia. Jane picked up a SS hat and it came flooding back, the night Yochana shot the

THE HURT OF YOCHANA

SS soldier. She suddenly started shaking and convulsing. Millie heard the noises Jane made and ran into the tent. The next thing Jane was on the floor throwing her arms and legs about as if she was having a fit.

"Call an ambulance please hurry." The antique seller called for an ambulance and by the time it arrived Jane appeared to be in a coma. Millie was holding her and comforting her. She was allowed in the ambulance with Jane and Jane was taken straight into intensive care. Millie stepped outside and tried to ring Jamie who was at the stag night in Prague but there appeared to be no signal. It went to answer phone so she left a message "Jamie call me as soon as you get this message. Jane is poorly, she is in intensive care and appears to have had some kind of seizure. Please call me"

THE HURT OF
YOCHANA

Millie waited and waited but Jamie never called. She didn't know the other lads very well so had no contact numbers for them. Jamie had said the hotel had been changed just before they left. He would text its name but there was nothing on her phone. This was so out of character for Jamie, he always worried when Millie was away. Millie went back and was met by the doctor.

"Are you next of kin?"

"Yes, I am now, my name is Mrs. Millie Trench." The doctor said his name was Silcott Boom

"Come into my office please Mrs. Trench and take a seat," and he pointed to a green leather chair. Millie sat down. Miss Egan is in a bad way. We are running tests and so until we know what has caused this we are as much in the dark as you."

"As she ever had any attacks like this before?"

"Not that I am aware of."

"Any history in her family of the convulsions?"

"Yes, her father Liam Egan had them."

"Which hospital did he attend?" Millie wrote down the address and handed it over to Dr. Boom.

"Thank you, this may help in our search for the answers. We have rooms for family members who are attending a seriously ill patient."

"Is Jane in that category Doctor?"

"I am afraid at the minute yes, she is. The nurse will show you to your suite Jane needs to rest and we also need to take blood samples I will contact her father's hospital to see what we can get from his notes." Millie tried another four times to get hold of Jamie without success. This is so bloody annoying she thought. It was 2.00am Monday morning when eventually Millie got a call from the house phone from Jamie.

"Hi Millie, sorry I haven't rung. I had my phone pinched two hours after landing. Are you having a nice time?"

"No Jamie I'm not having a nice time. Jane is in intensive care. She has had a seizure like Liam used to have."

"What?"

"There is so much going on in Jane's life. You best come up and I will tell you the full story."

"Right I am setting off now. Do you want some clothes bringing up?"

THE HURT OF
YOCHANA

"Bring enough clothes for another week." Millie then broke down.

"Hey steady on Millie, I will be with you in a few hours."

"I miss you," she said.

"Miss you too. I am on my way." Millie put the phone down she was so pleased Jamie was on his way. She didn't want to face this on her own.

Jamie and Millie spent the next few days by Jane's bedside while the doctors tried frantically to find the problem. It was Thursday morning at 10.00am when Jane woke. She appeared to have no lasting effects from the coma. Dr. Boom said all the exhaustive tests had come back negative. He explained to Jane, Jamie and Millie that this could have been a one off or the start of something more sinister.

THE HURT OF
YOCHANA

They thanked the doctor for his efforts and he signed the release for Jane to go home.

"You can come back with us for a few weeks Jane and build your strength up."

"I feel fine Uncle Jamie."

"Jane knows best Jamie."

"Whose side are you on Millie?"

Nobody's side, I just want what's best for Jane."

"Please don't fall out."

"We aren't Jane, just Uncle Jamie being a worry wart."

"Did anybody tell Jenny what happened?"

"Oh, crikey sorry Jane, I didn't think."

"I best call her." Jenny's phone was dead. Not like Jenny she thought. They arrived back and the house was in darkness.

THE HURT OF
YOCHANA

"Hello," Jane shouted down the hall, "Jen we are home." No answer.

"Doesn't look like she has come back from her friends in Stoke yet."

"Well I suppose that's good. She doesn't have to know about all this."

"Oh there's a letter here from Simpson the solicitor." Jane opened the letter.

"He wants me to go to the reading of Maria and Robert's will tomorrow at 11.00pm."

"I find this all strange Jane," said Uncle Jamie. Millie kicked him which made Jamie jump.

"I know Uncle Jamie. Has Aunty Millie told you everything?"

"Yes, she has sweetheart."

"Will you come with me to the reading tomorrow?"

THE HURT OF
YOCHANA

"I need to get back down London now you are ok," said Jamie

"Not a problem Jamie, I'll go with Jane."

After dinner, they watched a bit of TV then Jane said she was going to bed. Jane soon fell asleep. Millie checked on her then she and Jamie went to bed.

"I'm not happy about this Millie, this is going down a similar route as Liam."

"What can we do other than support her decisions Jamie?"

"I know, but she doesn't know all we know does she?"

"What and you think we should tell her now after what she has just been through?"

"No I don't Millie, but I would hate for her to fall out with us if she found out before we come clean."

THE HURT OF YOCHANA

"Would taking her to Nicola Gielbert be a good idea?"

"I really don't know Jamie. Look, let's get some sleep and see what tomorrow brings." The following day at breakfast Jamie asked Jane if she'd had anymore dreams. Jane said, "No they seem to have stopped since Maria died."

"That's good then sweetheart."

"Uncle Jamie, when dad was poorly was it the same as what I just had? Only I overheard the nurses talking about it." Jamie shuffled nervously on his chair.

"It sounds similar," he retorted. Just at that moment, as if on cue, Millie placed their breakfast on the table.

"There you go, and yes your egg is runny Mr. Trench," she said smiling. Jamie finished his breakfast and said his goodbyes. He turned to Jane, "You don't have to stay here. You can come down to us for a few months, it might just help."

"Thank you Uncle Jamie, but I want to do this course, I really do."

"Well we are here for you anytime day or night," and he pecked her on the cheek. He kissed Millie and left for his train.

Jane and Millie grabbed their coats and headed for the solicitors. On the way they passed Ringo's as it had affectionately become known as by the student fraternity.

"It's so sad that Robert took his own life Aunty Millie."

"I am afraid that's life Jane. You get to my age and things stop shocking you and I don't mean that in a nasty way either."

"I know Aunty Millie. I guess you become anesthetized to events the more you hear and see of them."

THE HURT OF
YOCHANA

"How did you sleep last night Jane?"

"Well I didn't dream Aunty Millie."

"Well let's hope that is the last of this for you." They arrived at the solicitors and were shown to Mr. Simpson's office.

"Please take seat ladies. I will now read the last will and testament of Maria Chayobbi Klinck and Robert Klinck. I was contacted by Robert and Maria a month ago with their wish to write a will. The following are the details of the Klincks.

I Maria Chayobbi Klinck am of sound mind and body on this date 12th September 2016. All my worldly goods and all my savings and personnel effects I leave to Jane Egan as gratitude for saving my dear sister all those years ago.

Mrs. Chayobbi Klinck's will amounted to savings with the Royal Bank of Scotland, Manchester Branch, of £47,300 and savings with the Liverpool Building Society to the sum total of £18,500. A property in Beatrice, Nebraska, once the family home of Mr. Klinck which now passes to you. All personal effects which amount to an inscribed wedding ring, a four diamond cluster engagement ring and a ruby and emerald eternity ring. Two watches; one a Longines and the other a Seiko. That is the full contents of Mrs. Chayobbi Klinck's will.

Last Will and Testament number two also to be read today by myself. This is the last Will and Testament of Robert Klinck. I am of sound mind and body on this date 12th September 2016. I Robert Klinck leave all my worldly goods to Jane Egan in recognition for making the last days of my mother's life happy in the sound knowledge that you came." At this point

even the solicitor looked puzzled and
Millie and Jane just looked at each other in
total bewilderment. "The following details
are what Robert betrothed to Miss Jane
Egan. The Café and all its contents
including the four bed accommodation and
the granny annex. My Mini Clubman
estate. My collection vinyl records. I wish
my clothes to go to a charity shop.

That Miss Egan concludes the last will
and testaments of both Maria Chayobbi
Klinck and Robert Klinck. I will need your
bank details to transfer any monies into
your account from this reading. I will also
need your address for transfer of the rest
of the items." Jane sat stunned like a rabbit
in the headlights of a car.

"I can't believe this Mr. Simpson. I
hardly knew them?"

THE HURT OF
YOCHANA

"Well you certainly made an impression. I did ask if you were a relative but apparently there are no living relatives. Maria just said she knew many years ago that you would come into her and Robert's lives. You are a wealthy young woman," and he got up and shook Jane's hand.

"I did a little research on the American property and it is a very big house so would possible be worth between $300,000 -$450.000. I would suggest you go and look at the property as soon as possible Miss Egan."

"I will Mr. Simpson." Jane wrote all her details down for Simpson.

"Just one other thing. We were instructed to arrange the funerals of Maria and Robert. Their request was for their funerals to be at St Stephens Church, Oakby Road, Liverpool. Because of the situation, I would imagine this will take at least a couple of weeks so I will be in touch. Is it ok if I call you, Miss Egan?"

"Yes, that's fine Mr. Simpson," and they both thanked him and left.

"Come on let's have a coffee here at Starbucks Jane, so you can gather yourself." Millie ordered two coffees and a cream cheese bagel each.

"Thank you, Aunty Millie. I don't know what to do I am in total shock."

"You will be sweetheart, you have just inherited a lot of money."

"The thing is, it just makes it worse. When Mum and Dad died they left me financially ok, but I still had the driving force to go to University. But now I have all this as well. I can't sell the shop, I feel that would be a betrayal of Robert and Maria what do you think?"

THE HURT OF
YOCHANA

"I think it's too early to be making life changing decisions."

"You are right Aunty Millie. I also feel dreadful because in my dreams I haven't saved Maria's sister, not even met her and since Maria died so have the dreams! I am thinking of delaying my course while I take time to visit America and sort the café out what do you think?"

"Jane, you are young enough to pick up your course in two years if you so wish, so I wouldn't make that a pressure for yourself."

"Aunty Millie I am so glad you came with me. Luckily in that shoe box are the recipes for Maria's cheesecakes."

"Ooh you must copy them for me, your Uncle Jamie loved them." They wandered around Liverpool and Jane tried again to contact Jenny but still her phone was dead.

THE HURT OF
YOCHANA

It was 9.30pm when they got back to the house. Jenny was home.

"What the hell happened to you?"

"I fell over."

"Was Simon with you?" Jenny hesitated.

"Yes, he picked me up."

"I have been trying to ring you, but had no joy."

"I smashed my phone as I fell Jane."

"Oh, mate you are in the wars."

"Where have you two been?" Jane sat down and told Jenny the full story about the Will and everything.

"Oh, I am so pleased for you Jane."

"Not sure you will be when I tell you what I am thinking about doing."

"What's that Jane?"

"Thinking of cancelling my course. I have to go to America to look at this property, and then I thought I would try and run Ringo's."

"Any jobs?" said Jenny.

"Are you joking?"

"No, I'm not really enjoying this course. If you wanted a hand to run the café, I could help you."

"Jen that would be brilliant. We could run it between us and there is loads of accommodation with it. I love baking Jen."

"Perfect then that's what we will do." Millie seemed a bit apprehensive at the girl's enthusiasm. It all seemed too sudden, but that's the young generation of today she thought. The two girls were very excited.

"Jane if you are ok, then I will get back tomorrow, unless you want me to do anything?"

THE HURT OF
YOCHANA

"No, you have been great Aunty Millie. I am going to see my course tutor and explain tomorrow. I think I will come down to London and stay with you and Uncle Jamie overnight, if that's ok. Then fly out to Nebraska the following day."

"Of course it's alright. You know Uncle Jamie will want to take you to the airport. Right I'm off to bed, all this excitement has made me tired. Goodnight Jenny, goodnight Jane."

"Yeah sleep tight," both girls shouted. Once Millie had gone to bed Jenny opened up to Jane.

"I didn't fall over Jane. Simon hit me."

"He what?"

"He hit me."

"Why would he do that Jenny?"

"Because I saw something I shouldn't have on his IPad."

THE HURT OF
YOCHANA

"What do you mean?"

"Well, we were having a coffee and a lady with a pushchair tried to get past and she knocked my coffee over Simon. I grabbed his IPad so that it wasn't in coffee. He had a message saying the Polish girls would arrive in Liverpool in one week's time and he was to put them to work straight away and 37% of the takings were his to use as he pleased."

"So why would he hit you."

"He spotted me reading it. I know I shouldn't, but when something catches your eye Jane."

"So then what happened?"

"He said he wanted to go for a walk to get some fresh air. He looked angry. We got just inside Sefton Park and he dragged me into the bush and started hitting me. He told me that if I ever told anybody about the email I had read, he would kill me and my family."

"Still not understanding why?"

"Simon is running a slave empire, bringing girls in from the Eastern Block with promises of jobs in hotels but they put them to work on the streets."

"Really, I can't believe this Jen."

"Did he tell you this Jen?"

"Yes, afterwards he made me go for a drink with him and he told me the full story. He was apologising for his actions by blaming it on what he was doing."

"Did he say Matt was doing it also?"

"Yes, he said he was involved."

"This all adds up when I saw Matt with that blonde girl in the canteen. We must go to the Police Jen."

THE HURT OF
YOCHANA

"No Jane he is in cahoots with some real dodgy people, I don't want to see him again."

"What about those poor girls Jane?"

"Listen to me I think the attacks on us two may have had something to do with all this."

"Please let's just forget and look forward to a new life. We are going to have so much fun Jane."

"Ok, it goes against my principles but there is just too much going on. Just keep away from him."

"Well if we are leaving University he won't know where we are unless somebody say's we are running the café."

"Listen why don't you tell your tutor same time I do tomorrow and then come down to London with me? We can stop at my Mum and Dad's old place. Then fly out to Nebraska to see this house I have been left."

"I would love to Jane, but to be honest I couldn't afford to. I have a bit saved up, but while we are getting the café off the ground I will need every penny."

"Don't be soft it's my treat and I could do with the company."

"Are you sure Jane?"

"I am more than sure."

"Ok let's do this. As a matter of interest where is Beatrice, Nebraska?"

"Do you know, I don't know. Let's look it up."

The girls got their laptops out and found the place to be in the Mid West of America.

"This is real cowboy country Jen."

"I am so excited Jane, it's like a whole new life is opening up for us both."

THE HURT OF YOCHANA

"Look Jen we have paid our rent on this for the next three months, so let go into University tomorrow and tell our tutors, then get the next train to London what do you reckon?"

"I'm off to pack now Jane, see you in the morning." Jenny left the kitchen and headed to the bedroom. Jane did the same. She packed some clothes and decided she better take the rose so she carefully packed the rose in the side compartment of her suitcase. Once packed she rang Aunty Millie and told her about her and Jenny's decision.

"So, you are coming down tomorrow? Uncle Jamie has booked for us to go away to Stratford for our wedding anniversary. We could cancel."

"Don't be daft Aunty Millie, I will see you when we get back from America."

THE HURT OF YOCHANA

"Ok love, just watch out for those cowboys," and she laughed. Jane cancelled the call and climbed into bed. She was soon fast asleep. There was no dreaming and when she woke the next morning she felt like a pressure had been lifted. Since Maria had died there had been no dreams, although the guilt was there with regard to Maria and her sister who she believed Yochana had saved. Jenny was already up and making them both bacon sandwiches.

"This is so exciting Jane I could hardly sleep. What about you, no dreams I hope?"

"No nothing Jen, it's like since Maria has passed they have stopped. She must have just been some kind of catalyst I guess."

THE HURT OF YOCHANA

The girls finished their sandwiches and decided to phone their tutors. Both girls got a bit of a grilling from their respective tutors, but there was nothing they could do to change their minds.

"Right let's get down to London and sort flights out to Nebraska Jen." Like a couple of giddy schoolgirls they left Liverpool for St Pancras station. They arrived at Jane's apartment at just after 6.00pm.

"Let's see what flights we can get Jen. It looks like they fly into a place called Omaha or a place called Lincoln."

"Which one is closest Jane?" asked Jenny.

"It looks like Lincoln, they have a flight from Gatwick at 9.05am in the morning with one stop in Chicago arriving at

THE HURT OF
YOCHANA

Lincoln for 7.09pm going tomorrow. Shall
we go for it Jen?"

"Fine by me." Jane booked the flight
and they ordered a take away. By the time
they had eaten it was almost 9.00pm.

"Jen I am going to bed. This time
tomorrow we will be in Beatrice, I hope
staying at the house."

"Don't forget the keys," Jane and Jenny
laughed.

"Yeah that would be a disaster if we
couldn't get in mate." They both headed
for bed. Jane lay for a while thinking
about what Maria had done for her and
what little she had done for Maria.
Eventually fell into a deep sleep. The
following morning their taxi arrived at
5.00am to take them to Gatwick.

"Did you dream last night Jane?"

THE HURT OF
YOCHANA

"Nothing again Jen, it's like a distant memory mate."

"Well I suppose that is good for your health at least Jane."

"I know you are right Jen but I just feel guilty for Maria's sister I am supposed to have saved and I don't even know her!"

"It is strange I agree, but just let it go." They settled down on the flight and although they had a short delay in Chicago the pilot made it up on the short flight to Lincoln. Lincoln was a small airport with one luggage carousel so while Jenny waited for their luggage Jane went to hire a car from one of the numerous car hire companies. Jenny grabbed the case and Jane led the way to the hire car.

"It's got a Sat Nav Jen, so we should be ok." Jane put in the zip code and it said it

THE HURT OF
YOCHANA

was thirty eight miles to the house. The roads were empty leaving Lincoln.

"Not like London hey Jen. I think we have only passed one car and we are twenty miles in to our destination." They eventually arrived at Beatrice and the house of Walter and Maria Klinck. It was a big imposing house painted white with a wrap round porch. The steps leading onto the porch had seen better days.

"Be careful Jenny they are a bit worn and slippery." Jane pushed the big old key into the lock of the front door and once inside felt round for a light switch. She flicked the light on and the sight they were to see took their breath away. The entrance hall and living room looked like it was in a time warp from just after the war. Everything was neat and tidy but covered in cob webs, the furniture was clearly quite expensive in its day and had worn well. The girls looked at each other, "I don't know what to say Jane," said Jenny.

"It must have been some place in its day." The girls set off round the house. The dining room was massive and there were pictures of Walter Klinck hanging on the walls in his American army uniform. There were some other pictures that looked like family members with a baby.

"I bet that's Walter Klinck, Jane, with his parents."

"Could be I guess." The kitchen still had a 1940's range in there and a big farmhouse table.

"Come on, let's go and see where we are sleeping tonight." They looked in the first room which again had the 1940's style furniture in it. Jane opened the door to the second bedroom and was shocked to find a freshly made bed and all the furniture was modern. There were two pictures, one either side of the bed. The first one was Walter and Maria they assumed, and the second one was Maria and another lady smiling. Jane picked it up and on the back it simply said Maria and Astera and a date 1937. They were both well dressed and the picture was in a beautiful garden.

"This is weird Jane, the whole house is in a time warp except for this room."

"Let's look at the others. If they are all covered in cobwebs, we will have to share the one decent room," and Jane laughed. The next bedroom had also been decorated and modern but there were no pictures in this one. "The other bedrooms were all in the time warp and covered in cob webs.

"Ok Jane you have the pictures room."

THE HURT OF YOCHANA

"Oh, thanks mate," and they both laughed.

"Let's get some sleep and look round tomorrow."

"Good idea Jane."

"Night, sleep well Jenny."

"You too mate."

Jane felt shattered after the journey and was soon in a deep sleep. The dream returned and she found herself as Yochana back in Deblun. The thread of the dream carried on. Yochana had seen Marsha murdered by the soldiers. They had no thought or conscience, they just treated the Jews like animals. How Yochana hated them. Mateusz, Yitzhak and Yochana hurried away and eventually arrived back at the safe house. Marsha's friend, the other girl in the house cried uncontrollably when Mateusz explained to everyone what happened.

"Let that be a lesson to all in this room," said Yitzhak. I put my arms round the girl and tried to comfort her. The girl said she was nineteen and she was from Bellonhoof close to the German border. She said her name was Alter and that her mother had given her that name because she was lucky to survive. She had been a very sickly child and the name Alter was like a blessing that she may live to an old age. She told me in a quietly spoken broken voice that Marsha and her parents were great friends. They had paid a man from the village to get them to England. She said he took the money and they had walked over 200 miles when he just disappeared. They decided to try and get to England themselves but were stopped

THE HURT OF
YOCHANA

just outside Deblun. She said the soldiers raped both her and Marsha. Then told them they were dirty little Jewish whores and they put them through the gates of Deblun. They said they would call and see them again one night. Altar was then physically sick, just telling the story had made her very ill. Yochana didn't know it at the time, but they would become good friends. Mateusz turned the lights out and they fell asleep.

The following morning Mateusz woke Yochana. He said because she was very slim she was to go with him and Yitzhak to steal food. There were never many people on the streets, only soldiers strategically placed. Nobody wanted to be seen by the Germans in case of reprisals. They had walked some seven miles when Mateusz pointed to a fence. He said across

THE HURT OF
YOCHANA

there was a hen farm. Yochana's job was
to steal eggs and he and Yitzhak would
kill the chickens but he said they had to be
quick because of the noise. Yochana could
feel her heart beating fast as they pushed
her under the wire and across some dirt
land until she got to the hen house. The
hens had just been fed and were already
quite noisy so that was lucky. She
gathered up about thirty eggs she thought.
Just as she was leaving the farmer saw her
and loaded his gun. He told her to put her
hands up but if she did all those lovely
eggs would smash on the floor. Because
she didn't do as he said he took aim. There
was a loud bang. Yochana had closed her
eyes thinking she was going to die but
when she opened them Yitzhak had shot
the farmer. He grabbed her arm.

THE HURT OF
YOCHANA

"Come on Yochana, we must hurry. The soldiers will have heard that shot." The three of us ran across the muddy field and Mateusz held up the wire for Yochana to crawl through. Once they were all on the other side of the fence Mateusz announced they would have to stay local for a couple of nights. There would be repercussions and whilst the German soldiers didn't know where they were they knew of this pocket of resistance.

About two miles from the farm they had just raided was a house that stood on its own.

"I know the man that owns this. I am sure he will let us stay, he and my father were friends." They arrived at the desolate house perched on a hill. Mateusz told them to wait by the big barn while he went to the door. The house was a white painted

THE HURT OF
YOCHANA

wooden house but the paint was more
yellow and brown now as it hadn't had
much care and attention for many years.
They could see from the barn an elderly
gentleman who opened the door. He flung
his arms round Mateusz and took him
inside. Twenty minutes passed before
Mateusz came onto the front porch and
gestured for them to go over to the house.
Mateusz introduced them to the old man.

"This is Leszek Zigurs, a dear friend of
my father's. We can stay here for a few
days until the heat dies down." Leszek was
about five feet eight, with grey shoulder
length hair and a grey moustache. He was
slightly stooped as if he had a spine
condition. Leszek told us to sit at the table
and he brought a bowl of Goulash for each
of us with bread, he said he had made. It
appeared that because of his isolated house

he was untouched by the outside world.
He told us that his wife had died many
years before and they had one son but he
had left to fight the Germans. Leszek
became emotional as he told us that he
didn't know if his boy was dead or alive.
He said he had begged him not to go but
he was strong headed and there was no
way he could stop him.

"Come with me," he said and he took us
to the old barn.

"Help me move these bales of hay
Mateusz." Under the hay bale was a trap
door and this led to a tunnel. The tunnel
must have been almost a mile long and
Leszek said it came out in the forest
beyond.

"My son built this for me," he proudly
declared. He told them, "If the Germans
come, they will burn the house and the

barn but they could escape. My boy always looked after me." Again Leszek got emotional. Mateusz comforted him and told him what a good lad he was. They sat in the makeshift tunnel while Mateusz told the old man why they were here and what he was doing. He told Leszek he would try and find out about his boy for him through his connections. They started to leave the tunnel to go back in the house. They could hear dogs barking. Mateusz told them to stay where they were. Leszek walked to the house and Mateusz stayed at the barn watching. Yochana could hear the German soldiers through the crack in the trap door. The Germans were asking if he had seen Jewish thieves. Of course Leszek said no. Against Mateusz's instructions Yochana and Yitzhak climbed out in to the barn. One of the German soldiers pulled

THE HURT OF
YOCHANA

out a hand gun and put it to Leszek's head
and said "Du dreckiger wenig liegende
Pol" Yochana knew what he had said
"You dirty little lying Pole." Yitzhak
grabbed Mateusz who was shocked to see
them.

"We can't help him, they will kill us all.
The Germans kept shouting, "Where are
they?" as they came out with the eggs and
the dead birds. Yochana held her breath,
praying Leszek would not reveal them.
The soldier with the gun then calmly shot
poor Leszek in the foot. He fell to the
ground in excruciating pain.   The soldiers
then all started kicking him.

"Torch the house," the German soldier
said, "and then the barn. If the Jews are in
there they will soon come out." Then
calmly and without a thought he shot
Leszek in the head. Mateusz had to be

restrained, "Come on," said Yitzhak, "We have to go." They scrambled into the tunnel just as the Germans threw lighted sticks into the barn. Yochana could feel the heat as she scrambled into the tunnel.

Jane woke from the dream. She had placed the plastic rose in a vase that was on the dressing table, now it was rolling about on the floor. The house had triggered her dreams again the sad thing was she was pleased. She wanted to find Maria's sister she believed she would then have peace. Jane left the bedroom and walked into the living room, Jenny was up and had removed the cream coloured blanket off one of the chairs and was sitting reading a book from the shelf.

"I could hear you scream Jane. I am assuming that your dreams have returned then?"

THE HURT OF YOCHANA

"Yes, they have Jen, I am quite pleased actually. Maybe then I can fulfill the wish of Maria and save her sister. What have you found to read?"

"It's really interesting. It appears Walter Klinck's father was a Hunkpapa Lakota North American Indian. It says here that he was with a hunting party in Porcupine Butte when they were stopped by the 7th US Cavalry and were herded to Wounded Knee. He said there were thirty eight braves in the hunting part of which he was one. His Indian name was Brave Bear. On the way to Wounded Knee the cavalry also rounded up some more Indians from the Miniconjou tribe which consisted of braves, women and children, and he just says old people. They were headed by Spotted Elk.

THE HURT OF
YOCHANA

On the way, he says that the cavalry were poking them and laughing at them calling them names. He said they arrived at Wounded Knee and made camp. They didn't know what their fate was going to be. The camp was surrounded by cavalry and he says there were four big guns at different places round the camp. He said Spotted Elk said it was no good to fight there was too many of them and that they were to do as they were told. The braves from Hunkpapa Lakota tribe asked Brave Bear to lead them against the cavalry.

They decided to break out on the evening of the high moon. Walter is writing this for his dad he puts in brackets December 29th 1890 Walter Klinck. Their plan wasn't to be. On the morning of December 29th the soldiers came and took all their weapons, until they got to an old

THE HURT OF
YOCHANA

Indian man who refused to give the
soldiers his rifle. A soldier shot the old
man then all hell broke loose. It says here
Brave Bear killed one of the soldiers with
his bare hands. With all the gun smoke
and the cannon fire he managed to get
away, picking up a young Indian girl
whose mother had been shot dead. It says
he walked from Wounded Knee with the
sixteen year old girl to Beatrice, Nebraska.
Walter puts in brackets 467 miles and
signs as if to verify. He said he fished and
hunted with his bare hands it took almost
twenty seven days to arrive in Beatrice.

When they arrived, just by chance, a
church missionary was riding in town in
his black buggy. He stopped and asked
Brave Bear where he was going. The
missionary understood some Indian and
they managed to communicate. The

missionary's name was Walter Klinck, a God-fearing man. He gave my father and Little River, the Indian girl, shelter and for my father work on the farm, also educating them at night. Eventually the missionary, Walter Klinck, died and left this house and some land to Brave Bear, who by now had married Little River. So, Brave Bear had a son in the fall of 1909 and he called him Walter Klinck after the missionary."

"Wow his whole life is a history lesson Jenny."

"I know isn't it interesting. Is there anymore Jen?"

"No, that's it. There are just cuttings about the massacre at Wounded Knee but no more explanations."

"I wonder what happened to the Indian squaw Little River."

THE HURT OF YOCHANA

"There is no more mention in this book."

"Come on let's go and discover the town." Beatrice had been quite a thriving town and head of Gage County. The main street sadly had seen better days, with the typical early 1900's type facades made of stone. Some had been painted to make them look more pleasant but it had only served to make things worse. The girls walked up Main Street. On one corner was a nursing home that looked like it had been a large hotel in its heyday. Further down was a bar called The Office.

"Shall we see if they do food Jen?"

"Come on then let's go in." They opened the wooden double doors with glass inlets saying The Office etched in the glass. Then there was a slatted pair of swing doors, the type you seen in the cowboy movies. Things didn't get much better inside. It was quite dark, there were three burly guys sitting at the bar with a beer and a chaser each. They wore bandanas on their heads and quite long beards, leather jackets with cut off denim jackets over them that looked like they needed a wash. On the back of the jackets was printed 'Nebraska Howling Wolf Chapter.' Jane looked at Jenny in despair. They were in now what did they do? The barman was a weasel of a man.

"What can I get you two pretty ladies then?" Jane saw her chance.

"Oh, we were just looking for food. I see you don't do it but thanks anyway," she said.

"Now listen to me little lady, I hear from that accent you ain't from these parts."

THE HURT OF
YOCHANA

"No, we are from England." At this one of the hairy bikers turned around.

"So, we have one of those English roses in the bar do we?" Jenny could feel her tummy tighten, they could just be in trouble.

"Two Jack Daniels and coke and two Fireballs for the ladies double quick." The little bar man scurried off.

"Actually, it was food we were wanting."

"Hey Mike you can do some food for these ladies can't you?" Clearly the barman was not allowed to say no.

"How do you fancy beef fries, with fries and beans?" Jenny and Jane felt they didn't have a choice so they said, "Yes that will be fine."

The big biker in the middle of the three stood up. He was a mountain of a man and

THE HURT OF
YOCHANA

he wandered over to the old Wurlitzer juke box in the corner. Suddenly Kid Rock was booming out and as he walked back. He grabbed Jenny and started to dance with her. Poor Jen didn't know what to do and Jane gave out a nervous laugh as he twirled her round.

"Give us a round again Mike," said the biker who had insisted Mike did the food. The song finished and they insisted that the girls sat with them at the bar. Jane was thinking bolt the food down and get the hell out of this place.

"So pretty ladies why are you in Beatrice?"

"You ain't here on holiday dude are you?" said the one biker who had yet to contribute any conversation.

"I have been left a house by Walter Klinck." The whole room went quiet.

THE HURT OF YOCHANA

"Have I said something wrong?" said Jane.

"You mean Walter Klinck of Beatrice?"

"Yes why?" All the bikers took off their bandanas and simply said, "Rest in peace, great man."

"Sorry to sound ignorant but why did you just do that?"

"Walter Klinck is a legend. He won the Medal of Honour for his bravery in World War Two when he was saving your asses."

"Really, are you kidding me?" said Jane.

"I kid you not sweet lady. Walter Klinck whose father was an Indian. Did you know that?"

"Yes, we read about that."

"Well young Walter was a mighty fine man and a hero, we must never forget that. You are safe in this town ladies any friend of Walter's is a friend of Beatrice." The food arrived and looked quite appetizing Jenny thought. They finished the meal and thanked the barman and the bikers. The noisiest Biker insisting on kissing each of the girl's hands and telling them "You get any hassle in this town, just tell them you are a friend of Cayote Bill, they won't bother you."

"Well thank you Cayote Bill. Been lovely to meet you. Oh I almost forgot what were the beef fries?" Bill let out a chuckle.

"Deep fried bull testicles my dear." Jane felt sick as she walked out but didn't want to seem ungracious.

"Wow Jane this is one hell of an adventure you have brought me on. Did you notice the quiet guy had a gun on his hip?

"Really, I didn't notice that Jen."

THE HURT OF
YOCHANA

"Where we going next?"

"I have instructions from the UK solicitor. We have to go and sign some papers at a US solicitor for the house."

"Where is it?"

"It says Vanover Solicitors, Garfield Street. Let's ask that sheriff." They wandered off to the sheriff parked outside a small hairdressers on Main Street.

"Excuse me officer."

"Good afternoon ladies, with an accent like that are you from Europe?"

"England actually."

"Wow my great granddaddy was from Yorkshire, England. Do you know it?"

"What Yorkshire? It's a county in England."

"You might know the Marshall's. My great aunt Peggy still lives there." Jenny looked at Jane they were both thinking why or how would they know this man's relations. They politely said they didn't.

"Well how can I help you? My name's Steve by the way." Steve was a good-looking man and Jenny was a sucker for a uniform. She was staring at him all googly eyed. Jane had to nudge her.

"We are looking for Vanover Solicitors on Garfield Street."

"Get in ladies, I will take you." As they drove across town the officer was grilling them on why they were in Beatrice. Jenny couldn't say anything, she was transfixed.

"Well there you go ladies. Good luck and hope to see you around." Jenny blurted, "Well I really hope so officer," as Jane thanked him and she pulled Jenny away.

"What is wrong with you Jen?" Jane said as they climbed the steps of what looked like a converted house. On the wall by the entrance was a brass plaque. It said Lori Ann Vanover lawyer then a string of letters below her name. They entered the reception area. A young girl took their details and said Miss Vanover would see them shortly and would they like to take a seat. After ten minutes Miss Vanover came down the stairs. She was about thirty three years old Jane thought. She was dressed in a white blouse and a brown pencil skirt set just above her knee with brown high heels. She was well spoken although she still had a Mid-Western drawl Jane thought.

"Lori Ann Vanover, pleased to meet you Miss Egan." She then looked at Jenny.

"Oh, sorry Miss Vanover, this is my friend Jenny."

THE HURT OF
YOCHANA

"Very pleased to meet you both, I adore your accents. Please follow me." The girls were shown upstairs to a small office.

"Ok so you are here about your inheritance Miss Egan."

"Yes, please call me Jane."

"Then you must call me Lori, Jane."

"I don't know how much you know about your friend Walter Klinck?"

"Just some of the things we read at the house."

"Well let me enlighten you. The original Walter Klinck came from Germany and settled in Beatrice, Nebraska and was one of the founding fathers of our town. Old Walter, as we call him, was a missionary and was given the land that the house you have inherited stands on by the US government, who were trying to get people to stay in the Mid West. Walter

became a well-respected God fearing man
and slowly bought land surrounding the
house which he built to the size it is today.
One day, while he was out in his buggy he
came across an Indian brave called Brave
Bear with a squaw called Little River.

Walter never told anyone other than
some very close friends that the Indians he
had taken under his roof had been at the
Wounded Knee massacre. He was fearful
of retribution for them. He educated Brave
Bear and Little River and they became
citizens. We Nebraskans like nice people,
we have no prejudice. I think this was
because it was so hard to survive in the
early days, that had to help each other.
Anyway, I digress. When Old Walter
passed on the estate was left to young
Brave Bear. He married Little River and
their only child was born and he named

him Walter, after the man he loved so much.

Young Walter was a great athlete and excelled. When his country came calling he joined up. In December 1941 four days after the bombing of Pearl Harbour America committed totally to the war effort.

In May 1942 Walter was fighting in a small town near the Egyptian border when three of his colleagues came under heavy fire and were badly wounded. They were Sergeant Eggert, Corporal Gillespie and Sergeant Major Knapp. Seeing what had happened Walter Klinck left his post and managed to carry Eggert first, then Gillespie second back to safety. Although badly shot they did survive. His commanding officers ordered him to stay where he was, as it was fruitless, Sergeant

THE HURT OF
YOCHANA

Major Knapp was probably dead now
anyway. Being from Indian stock, his
father and mother taught him Indian ways
as well as the American ways. They taught
him to respect nature and people. Young
Walter could not have lived with himself
so he disobeyed his officer, and scrambled
back under heavy fire. He picked up all
three men's rifles and Sergeant Major
Knapp and brought them to safety.

His commanding officer did give him a
dressing down for disobeying an order but
didn't put that in his report and Walter was
given the Medal of Honour by the
President Franklin D Roosevelt at the
White House. Young Walter was a quiet
man, and to be honest when he settled in
England people round these parts were not
surprised. I don't think Walter could
handle the adulation. His medal which as

part of his estate is now yours." Jane could feel herself welling up. Just then Lori said something that would haunt Jane.

"I know this might sound strange, but with your olive skin you could be mistaken for a North American Indian." Jane smiled.

"What happened to Little River nobody knows. Apparently, again this is hear-say, Walter wrote telling his mother he was marrying and settling in England. They say that day she packed a small bag, locked the door to the house, left a key with a neighbour, and was never seen or heard of again. They say she was broken hearted that she thought Young Walter would come back to her. Bit sad I guess girls. Walter and Maria did come to live here for a short time and young Walter tried to find his mother but she had gone and sadly Walter left to make a life with Maria in England."

"Ok so the house is yours. Please sign here. The medal is yours. I took the liberty of having the house valued for you by a local reality agent. They say because of the significance and the history of the property and the people who lived there it is valued at $435,000. That is very high for this state Jane. If you were not a rich lady before you are now. What is the connection between you and Young Walter?"

"This is terrible," Jane said. "I will try and explain." It took Jane almost an hour to go through how this all happened.

"Look Jane, Jenny do you fancy a night out in Wilbur?"

"What's Wilbur?"

THE HURT OF
YOCHANA

"It's the Czechoslovakian capital of America. Great little town with a couple of bars."

"How do we get there?"

"My friends husband is taking us and bringing us back so sure he wouldn't mind a couple of limeys," and she laughed showing her extra white teeth.

"Great, what time?"

"We will pick you up from the house at say 8.00pm." Jenny and Jane thanked Lori and headed back to the Klinck house.

"What a flippin' strange day Jen."

"I know, can't believe you took me to a Hells Angels bar, then we find all this stuff out about Walter Klinck. Sounds like he was some man, eh Jane."

"Looking forward to tonight Jen, are you?"

THE HURT OF
YOCHANA

"Can't come quick enough Jane, Lori seems like a really nice girl? Everyone we have met so far seem really nice people Jane."

It was soon 8.00pm and a car pulled up outside of the Klinck house.

"Come on Jen, Lori is here." They climbed in the back. A dark-haired guy with swarthy looks and a baseball cap with sun glasses perched on the back of the hat turned.

"Nice to meet you ladies I'm Scott Holcombe."

"Nice to meet you Scott Holcombe," Jenny said and Jane smiled.

"So you ladies are hitting the hotspots of Wilbur eh?"

"Take no notice," Lori said, "he is just having a bit of fun. Flippin' drive Holcombe." Everyone laughed. They arrived passing over a railway line to the town called Wilbur. It looked fairly prosperous but they were beginning to realise that all the towns in the Mid West had this cowboy type town feel to them and Wilbur was no exception.

Lori, Jane and Jenny entered the first bar. It actually had swing doors and a long saloon bar. One old girl was serving and there were about twenty people in the bar of varying age groups.

"Don't worry, will just have a warm up few beers here, then go across the road to the Texas Tart bar."

"That sound interesting Lori."

"It's a good night tonight, sure you will enjoy it girls." They all had what Lori said was Captain Morgan's Rum with skinny coke; doubles which were more like trebles as they were free pour. Jane's eye surrounded the interior which the walls had green and gold flock paper and wooden floor boards. She expected Clint Eastwood to come strolling in at any minute.

"This is great Lori," said Jane.

"So, have you thought anymore about the house and what you might do?"

"I really don't know. I thought how sad. I feel for Little River. I suppose she will be long gone by now."

"Just a bit Jane, she would be almost one hundred and forty years old," and Lori laughed.

"Duh sorry, just not thinking."

"Only joking Jane, another round?"

"Why not hey Jenny?"

"I'll go and order while you two have a chinwag."

THE HURT OF
YOCHANA

"Jane I don't want to upset you or anything but that house is pretty much a no go area for people in Beatrice."

"What do you mean?"

"Well if you are thinking of selling, I would advertise out of the County."

"Why is that then?"

"People say Little River haunts the house. All a load of bunkum Jane but I think you would struggle. I have a friend in Lincoln County. I could contact her Realty Agency and handle it this end for you."

"How much do you charge?"

"Well we usual take a 12.5% fee but seeing that hopefully we will become friends I would do it for 7.5%."

"Do it then Lori. I can't see the point in having a property over here. I was left the café and things and my parents also left me an apartment in London when they died."

"Oh, I am sorry to hear you have lost your parents, were they quite young?"

"Yes, they were."

"Sorry to hear that Jane." Just then Jenny arrived with the drinks on a tray.

"Come on girls one, two, three let's go sailing with the captain. It was 10.57pm when the girls left the bar to go across to the Texas Tart.

"Evening ladies," said two burly men in their mid thirties both wearing cowboy hats. Jane was feeling quite drunk and Jenny said she was the same. Lori seemed to be ok. The Texas Tart bar had a live band and a disco. When the girls arrived the band were just finishing their last spot.

"Whooo," Lori shouted, "Same again girls?" and she ordered three rum and skinny cokes. They managed to find a seat and a table. A tall guy in a cream cowboy hat came over and sat with them.

"Oh girls this is Dan Manley."

"You are certainly that," said Jane who now was trying to recover herself, straightening her hair and smiling at Dan.

"Say you are one pretty lady there darlin'. Are you from Ireland? You look like you have some Native American in you sweet-cheeks." Jane blushed. Not wanting to be left playing the wallflower Jenny introduced herself and said, "We are both from England."

Dan smiled at Jenny but only had eyes for Jane.

"You going to have a dance with me sweet-cheeks?" The disco was playing Dr. Hook 'I'm going to love you a little bit more'. Jane was quite like her mum in stature, so quite tall but Dan towered over her.

As he held her close she remembered thinking, is this love at first sight that people talk about? For the rest of the night they danced and talked. It was 2.00am when Scott came to pick them up. Jane kissed Dan goodnight and climbed into the back of Scott's car.

"Well one of you looks like you had a goodnight, am I right Jane?"

"You are 100% right. He isn't married or anything is he Lori?"

"No I have been friends with Dan since high school. He is a really lovely guy Jane." Scott dropped Jane and Jenny off at the house and Jane said she would pop by to Lori's office later that day to sign the paperwork to sort the house sale out.

THE HURT OF
YOCHANA

"Jen I can't believe it, he is flippin' gorgeous I have fallen for him in a big way."

"It's time you had some good luck mate," said Jenny.

"Right I'm off to bed I could sleep on a washing line I'm that tired."

"Ok goodnight Jen." Jane went in her room and settled down under the duvet, her mind racing about Dan. Eventually the she fell sound asleep. The first thing she remembered was she was feeling ill at ease she could hear a voice saying "They will pay" over and over again. This wasn't like the other dreams. She felt like an evil force was driving through her body as she was dreaming. Her dream then picked up where it left off.

They were climbing out of the tunnel which brought them into the wood. They

could hear German soldiers shouting and
dogs barking as they made their way back
to the safe house in Deblun. They arrived
back but there was nobody in the house.
The locks had been broken off, so the
Germans had found the house Mateusz
thought.

"Now what? Said Yitzhak.

"We need to get to the next town of
Bolaf. We have a safe house and
resistance there, we will be safe."

"Mateusz are you blind?" said Yitzhak
"They have locked down the town, there
are Germans everywhere."

"It is our only chance Yitzhak, we have
to try." Yochana felt very vulnerable at
this time, the two men she thought would
look after her were now arguing and for
the first time she could see Mateusz
wasn't confident.

THE HURT OF
YOCHANA

"We wait until early morning when the soldiers are skiving and not watching, then we make our move. Its two miles West to Bolaf," said Mateusz. They went into the now empty safe house there was blood up the walls

It looked like they may have butchered the rest of the group.

"This is why we have to go Yitzhak. We can't stay in this town."

"I know my friend but the reality is our chances are slim," said Yitzhak. It was 2.00am when they made their move, darting down alleyways keeping out of open spaces. Yitzhak wasn't wrong, there were Germans everywhere. It took almost four hours to travel the two miles distance from the town to the fence that separated the town of Bolaf.

"Now what Mateusz?"

THE HURT OF
YOCHANA

"We have very little time. Dig and keep digging with our bare hands. It is coming light now so we have to hurry." They frantically started digging with their hands. Luckily the ground wasn't frozen and had very little stones, so the first part was dug by 7.00am. Yitzhak got in the hole to dig under the fence to get to the other side. Yitzhak had almost done it when we could hear German soldiers and dogs. Yitzhak shouted Mateusz, "You have to hide."

"I am keeping digging Mateusz, it's our only hope. Good luck my friend," and Mateusz grabbed Yochana by the arm and made her run to the woods. In the woods was a small stream which Mateusz said they were to submerge into, and then get across because the dogs would lose their scent. Yochana followed what Mateusz said. It was so cold she was at the point of thinking they can kill her. She wasn't sure she could go on. As they got out of the stream they heard the soldiers. They had caught Yitzhak and were asking him where his friends were. Yitzhak was so brave he said he was alone. They could hear them mercilessly beating him but he would not give them up. Finally they heard the officer tell Yitzhak that this was his last chance and he would blow his brains out unless he gave his friends up. Poor Yitzhak still said he was alone. They heard the gunshot. Tears trickled down her cold shaking face. Mateusz slapped her, "Stop this, you have to be strong if we are to survive. Yitzhak made his choice." The aggression in Mateusz voice resonated with her. He was hurting and this was his defense mechanism.

THE HURT OF
YOCHANA

It went quiet and it looked like the Germans believed Yitzhak and he had saved their lives.

"Now what do we do Mateusz?"

"We lie low until nightfall." Mateusz cuddled her and they tried to keep warm by holding each other. Yochana felt so wretched and hated the Germans so much for what they had done to her family and for what they were doing to the Jewish race. It was 2.00am when Mateusz woke her to say it was time for them to try and get to Bolaf.

"Where did you get the shovel from Mateusz?"

"I have my way's Yochana," he replied.

"Come on, we have very little time." They found an area of the fence that Mateusz said would be the best place to dig. He furiously dug away until eventually he had made a significant gap for them both to clamber under. Mateusz then scrapped the soil back in the hole and threw twigs and leaves to disguise their escape. There was more woodland to go through before they came to a clearing. It was starting to get light as they neared what Mateusz said was a safe house. Two burly men shook his hands and welcomed them.

"This is Yanni." Yanni was blonde with a small moustache which brought a smile to Yochana's face for some reason. Yanni shook her hand.

"This is Indris." Indris was quite surly and seemed to view Yochana with some apprehension although he did shake her hand.

"Come," said Yanni, "we have some fine soup and bread for you."

THE HURT OF YOCHANA

Jane woke from her dream totally in a daze. She could hear somebody in the kitchen.

"Hello," she shouted.

"You are up then Jane?"

"What time is it Jenny?"

"You have missed yesterday totally I couldn't wake you. I am guessing you have been dreaming again."

"Yes," and Jane started to tell Jenny all about her dream.

"Dan Manley called round. I didn't know what to say, so I said you had gone shopping. I couldn't say you had been asleep thirty six hours, could I?" and Jenny laughed.

"Suppose you are right. Oh blimey I was meant to go and see Lori."

THE HURT OF YOCHANA

"Yes she rang your mobile so I answered and told her you would be in today. To be honest I wasn't sure you would be awake," which brought more laughter from the pair.

"Don't laugh at me Jen but I think I have fallen for Dan in a big way."

"You looked as if you were smitten mate."

"We go back tomorrow. Should I tell him?"

"Well they say faint heart never won fair lady, in this case gentleman mate," said Jenny.

"Come on we best get down to Lori's and get these papers signed." With all the legal work done with Lori Jane phoned Dan. He said to meet him at a bar called the Rail. Jane and Jenny went to the Rail and Jenny made herself scarce while they talked. After about half an hour Jane excitedly stood up and shouted Jenny over.

"We are getting engaged and Dan is coming over next week. He works for Kawasaki so he is pretty sure he can get a transfer to their Liverpool factory." Jenny looked at Jane in amazement but didn't want to spoil the day, although she thought it all seemed a bit rushed to say the least.

"Mate I am so happy, Dan is such a lovely guy." Jenny could not hold her concern any longer.

"Jane please don't think I am being spiteful or anything, but you really don't know this guy do you?"

"They say some people fallen in love instantly and I think we have Jen." Jenny realised nothing would change her friend's mind so she left it at that.

THE HURT OF
YOCHANA

Once back at the house Jane phoned
Millie and told her about what she had
decided with the house, then she dropped
the bombshell about Dan and the
engagement. Millie was shocked but
realizing how happy Jane seemed she
decided that the least said was soonest
mended.

"Can I come and stay for a couple of
weeks Aunty Millie and can Dan stay
also?"

"I would love you too meet him and
show him London."

"Do you know Aunty Millie, he has
never seen an ocean." Jane then told Millie
about the plan for the café and for Dan to
move with his company. Millie wasn't
sure what to say but she knew Jamie
would be livid.

THE HURT OF
YOCHANA

Jane came off the phone and the girls decided it had been such a rushed day that they would have an early night before flying back. Before they went to bed Jenny asked a question.

"Can I go to the café and live Jane?"

"Of course mate. Why not advertise for some staff and let's say we will re-open in a month. I should be back in Liverpool by then." Before they went to bed Jane said, "Do you know what mate I feel bloated."

"You must be pregnant," Jenny said and laughed.

Flippin' heck Jen, we only did it the once, me and Matt Babington, and to be honest that was my first time."

"I was only joking Jane. I know but it would be a bit ironic eh?"

The girls made their way to bed. Jane was soon asleep again and the dream started. Jenny was reading when she heard a loud bang she got up and shouted to Jane. There was no reply so Jenny went into Jane's bedroom. She found Jane rolling about on the floor as if she was having a fit. Poor Jenny didn't know what to do so she ran to the nearest house and an elderly couple called for the medics.

Jane was rushed to Lincoln General Hospital. Jenny phoned Millie and explained what had happened and she said she would be on the next flight. Jenny then phoned Lori and Dan they all met at the hospital. Poor Jane had gone into a coma and was unaware of what was happening, in the dream world she was back in Bolaf.

As Yochana and Mateusz enjoyed the hot soup that Yanni and Indris had given them there was suddenly a loud banging on the door. Yanni turned to Mateusz, "It's the German death squads they are rounding up elderly and shooting them in Berkof wood. Quick get in the loft." Only Indris stayed. They heard him open the door. The German shouted at him Jewish pig are you on your own? Indris replied that he was.

"Then you need to come with us." Yochana held Mateusz back. He knew what was Indris's fate should he leave with them. Suddenly a scream was heard.

"He stabbed me," said the German soldier.

"The Jewish pig stabbed me in my eye." Suddenly there was massive commotion and they heard several shots. Then it went quiet and they thought they were going but one of the soldiers said, "Look this soup is hot, and the table is set for four pigs."

THE HURT OF
YOCHANA

"Search the house," the commanding officer shouted. It wasn't long before they found them. They were told to put their hands on our heads. There were three soldiers and one officer. They pushed Yochana on a table and were about to rape her. They were all laughing. Yochana was crying and pleading with them to stop. Mateusz could stand it no more. He grabbed the gun of the officer and shot him and two more of the soldiers. The third soldier tried to get away but Yanni broke his neck.

"Come on get their clothes off them and we will walk out of here using Yochana as a decoy. Hurry, hurry," shouted Mateusz. Yanni put on the tallest German soldier's uniform and Mateusz put on the officer's. Luckily Mateusz could speak German. They locked the door leaving all the dead bodies in the house. Yochana noticed Yanni kissed Indris's dead body and closed his eye lids before they left. Once outside Mateusz commandeered a car he said Yochana was resistance and he was taking her to Deblun for interrogation. They drove out of the gates, it was that easy. As they were leaving German soldiers were herding young children, women and the elderly to a wood where they would be lined up and shot.

Mateusz said we had to decide what we wanted as we probably only had four hours before we would be discovered. We decided to try and head for Holland. Yanni said he had family there that might be able to get them to England.

Back in Nebraska, Millie had arrived at the hospital. Jenny said the doctor wanted to talk to Millie alone as she was the closest family member. Millie was shown into a small office and the doctor explained what he thought was happening to Jane.

"I am Mark Small, Senior Doctor, at this hospital." Millie put out her hand, "I am Millie Trench.

"Jane Egan appears to have had a seizure and her body has gone into shutdown," said Doctor Small.

"Do you know if any of her family have had this condition?" Millie explained about Jane's father, Liam Egan. But she said they never knew what caused it other than it came and went.

"Mrs. Trench, I have worked in this field for many years and trauma like this is quite uncommon with somebody so young. It is quite often brought on by a massive shock when your body then shuts down to protect you."

"Is she in pain doctor?"

"No, she is absolutely fine and we have monitored the baby." Millie looked at the doctor in shock, "The baby?"

"I am sorry, did you not know she is about fourteen week's pregnant?"

"Doctor, I would prefer we kept this part to ourselves."

"But of course Mrs. Trench, what is said in this room is for your ears only."

"Can the baby survive doctor?"

"I have no doubts the baby can survive, she is in the best place."

"What about Jane when will she come out of the coma?"

"I am sorry Mrs. Trench, but I can't give you a definitive answer. Jane may stay in this state for a very long time or she may come round tomorrow, we really don't know. We will be doing tests and a scan on her brain over the next few days and may know more then. But until we have carried out the tests I really can't give you any hope. My suggestion would be go home and visit as you wish. Where are you staying Mrs. Trench?"

"Jane is over here with her friend Jenny Makepeace, so I will probably stay with Jenny."

"Ok, well leave your cell phone number with the nurse so that we can contact you in case of any change."

Millie, Jenny and Dan left the hospital. Dan made his excuses and left them at the house. Millie got the impression that Dan would not be around, he hadn't signed up for this she thought. While Millie and Jenny sorted out what was to be done Jane

THE HURT OF
YOCHANA

was still dreaming and in the world of Yochana.

Yanni, Mateusz and Yochana headed down the country lanes for almost two hundred miles and then they ran out of fuel so abandoned the car. They headed for a dense wood. It was daylight so they needed to get undercover.

Yochana was about to discover the total horror and brutality of the war, Mateusz said to be quiet. As they walked they could hear gun fire. They scrambled to the top of a small incline and below they could see where some Jews had been made to dig graves and men, women and children were being lined up and shot, Yochana whispered to Mateusz that she knew the woman with the long dark hair, she was a family friend. They were

THE HURT OF
YOCHANA

dressed in jackets with the Star of David on the front and the word Jew on the back. The soldiers systematically and with no feeling shot what must have been three hundred human beings. The Jews that were left were told to cover the bodies and make good the ground. The soldiers then left leaving just two soldiers to watch over the work. Yochana felt every emotion, anger, hurt and hatred. Worse was to come. A small non-descript man with a limp and no teeth arrived with a horse and cart and the men making good the ground were told to strip the dead bodies and put the clothes on the cart. Yanni, Mateusz and Yochana watched in disgust as the soldiers took payment for the dead Jew's clothes. Yanni turned to Mateusz.

"I have had enough and he ran down the banking like a wild banshee quickly

THE HURT OF
YOCHANA

followed by Mateusz. They attacked the two guards killing them with their bare hands. They then kicked them into the man made grave. By now the remaining Jews had attacked and killed the horse and cart man and he also went in the grave. Mateusz spoke first. He pointed to the horse and cart, "Take this and go," he said to the three surviving Jews.

"We are taking the guns," said Mateusz. They didn't need to be told twice and they quickly moved the horse and cart. Now they had some guns and Yochana could tell Mateusz and Yanni felt better.

"Come on we must move quickly." They walked through the forest at a fast pace arriving near a town called Lavale. They were still unsure of where they were.

"Shh," said Yanni they could hear somebody walking on the forest floor.

THE HURT OF
YOCHANA

From the distance they could see an old woman with a shot gun and a mangy dog. Yanni gestured to get down behind some bushes, Yanni waited until the women had just gone past the bush and he jumped her knocking her to the ground while putting his hand over her mouth and his gun to her head. The little mangy dog just sat next to her owner. Yanni explained they would not hurt her but they needed food and water. The old lady nodded meaning she understood. It all calmed down and the lady said they were on the Dutch border and she pointed.

"Look," she said, "Amino." Yochana had heard of Amino when she was at school and knew it was a border town. The old lady now seemed relaxed, she wasn't going to be killed. She said she would feed thm and give them clothes, food and drink to take on their way. Yochana felt they now had a chance. Mateusz seemed happy with the situation but Yochana wasn't as sure as Yanni was as they walked down a farm track to a desolate farm house.

They needed provisions and clothes to take with them. The old lady said they should rest for the night as she climbed the stairs to her bedroom. They settled down then Yanni voiced his concerns.

"She is not what she seems Mateusz," he said.

"Why what is the matter?"

"I sense something." It was day break when they heard a clicking noise coming from upstairs. Yochana quietly stepped up the old creaky stairs and very slowly turned the door knob to the old lady's bedroom. She was sat at her dressing table sending a message. She looked startled.

THE HURT OF
YOCHANA

"Who are you contacting Yochana said? The old lady looked at her and paused for a few seconds.

"I am sending a message to my cousin to see if they can contact the Dutch resistance for you."

"Let me see," Yochana said. She was reluctant. Yochana's heart started beating fast, the old lady was contacting the Gestapo about them.

"How much have you sent of this message?" Yochana said. The old lady cowered, "Please don't hurt me, the Germans make me do it." Just then Yanni came in.

"What's going on?" Yochana told him.

"You witch I knew I couldn't trust you," he pulled out the gun and shot her. She fell back on the bed in a pool of blood.

THE HURT OF YOCHANA

"Come on Yochana, Mateusz," he shouted as we ran downstairs. It was too late, Mateusz was standing in the kitchen with his hands on his head surrounded by six soldiers and a gun to his head.

"Get here Jewish scum," said the commanding officer. He pulled Yochana by her hair it hurt so much. He then turned to Yanni.

"Have you killed our spy, Jewish pig?" Yanni knew what was coming and went for his gun but three of the soldiers opened their guns on him and he dropped dead in a pool of blood.

"Now you two, let's see where we can take you. Mateusz was thrown in the back of one truck and Yochana was thrown in the back of another. Yochana feared this was the end for her.

THE HURT OF
YOCHANA

Yochana's truck was full of women. There was nowhere to sit, they sort of half stood and half knelt down. Women were crying and one woman was dead. They used her to sit on. Yochana couldn't do this. She was not going to let the Germans take her dignity away. They travelled for three days with no food and just a small amount of water each time they stopped to fuel the truck.

Eventually at dawn they came to a crossing. Yochana could just see the sign it said Bridenbuf. Next the soldiers got out of the trucks and started herding them like cattle toward an iron gate above the gate it said "IN IHRER ARBEIT GLUKICH SEIN". It meant Be Happy in Your Work. Yochana felt some small relief that it appeared they would not be killed as this appeared to be a factory.

THE HURT OF
YOCHANA

A stern looking German soldier stood with a stick as he counted sixty people into the shed Yochana was allocated, which was Shed number four. There were rows of wooden bunk beds. Yochana shared her bunk bed with a girl called Astera. Astera was a slight girl and she said she had been there for what she thought was about six months. She told Yochana, "The only way to survive is to work hard, then the guards don't mistreat you and sometimes you may get a bit more stale bread. Those that don't work were quite often rounded up and we never see them again but the stench from the chimneys is disgusting."

Back in Jane's world time had moved on and she remained in a coma following the seizure. She had given birth to a little boy that Millie and Jamie had called Daniel Liam Egan. Fourteen years had passed and Danny, as he was now called, had become a big lad towering over Millie. Millie and Jamie had brought Daniel up, but tragedy struck when Daniel was three. Jamie had been coming home from work on his bike and a London bus hit him killing him outright. Millie had assumed the role of looking after Daniel. She would not let social services take him into care.

Daniel and Millie went every Saturday to the hospital. Jamie had paid for Jane to be brought home many years before and she was in King Edwards hospital. Every weekend Millie hoped for just a flicker of hope but nothing. Jenny had looked after the café in Liverpool and had married the man who delivered supplies from the warehouse. Millie tried to get up and see Jenny at least four times a year. Jenny was very happy and had twin girls who by now were twelve years old.

It was mid-day when Millie got a call from Jenny she seemed anxious.

"Millie is there any chance you can come up and see me?"

"Of course, what's the matter?"

"I will tell you when you get here." It was quite fortuitous Danny was on a skiing holiday in Austria with his school, so she got the next train up to Liverpool and Jenny met her at the station.

"You ok Jenny?"

"I'm not sure Millie. Remember when I cleared the flat that me and Jane shared before we went to America?"

"Yes, what about it Jen?"

"Jane was quite a tidy person so everything was in boxes and I never looked inside them, they were personal to

THE HURT OF YOCHANA

Jane I thought. Yesterday one of the twins
wanted to look in the loft for her cuddly
toys we bought years before. The loft is
safe, there is a proper ladder up to it and
floorboards, so I know she is safe.
Anyway, Clodagh that's the daughter in
the loft had been up there probably ten
minutes when I heard her scream. I ran to
the bottom of the loft steps and shouted up
to her. Clodagh appeared at the hatch and
she was white. I rushed up and held her
and she started crying. When I asked her
what had happened she wouldn't tell me. I
went into the loft and Jenny's plastic rose
and vase were rolling about on the floor.

I sat Clodagh down in the kitchen and
asked her if she had been in Aunty Jane's
things. She said she only looked but she
had picked up the vase and the rose.
That's when she said she saw an old

woman who was whispering "They must pay." I remembered Jane telling me that was what Maria Klinck had said to her in the café. It's pretty much spooked me out. Anyway, that night when I told my husband what had happened he laughed at me but said he would go into the loft with me. I was probably wrong doing this but I looked in Jane's boxes and I found this. Jenny produced an A4 book. I carefully opened to the first page and Jane had written this:

'I met Maria Klinck today at Ringo's café what an extraordinary lady,' and she dated that paragraph. All through the books she is documenting her dreams until the night she fell into a coma."

Millie could feel a coldness run down her spine. Should she tell Jenny about Jane's father and the dreams diary? She thought it was best not to saying anything as she had never told Jane the full extent of Liam's torment. It appeared that history was repeating itself. How I wish my Jamie was here Millie thought.

"This is so weird Millie what can we do?"

"Not a lot Jenny just get on with our lives and hope Jane comes back to us someday."

"But what is the significance of the red rose and the vase Millie?"

"I honestly don't know Jen, but maybe this is how Maria Klinck is communicating perhaps."

"Sorry Millie, I didn't ask how Jane was I am so wrapped up in all this."

"Just the same as she has been for the last fourteen years Jen. The doctors say they are baffled. They think she is in some kind of suspended dream state. They think she will come out of it but don't know where or when. As they sat sipping their coffees and catching up Millie's mobile rang it was the hospital.

"Hello," said Millie, "is everything ok?"

"I have good news for you Mrs. Trench, Jane is awake and talking. We will need to do some test but so far she looks fine. I haven't mentioned her son or that you have lost your husband."

"No that's great, this is such good news. Please tell Jane I will be there to see her first thing in the morning."

"Millie who is that?" Jenny asked. Millie just broke down and cried.

"Millie, are you ok?"

"Oh Jenny, Jane is out of the coma and they think she will be ok." Both women were now in tears.

THE HURT OF YOCHANA

"Right I'm shutting tomorrow and coming to London with you to see Jane."

"Jenny, please don't take this the wrong way but I have to introduce Jane to her son and also tell her about Jamie. Would you mind coming the following day?"

"Millie I wasn't thinking, I was so excited she is doing well. Of course you need some time with her. I will come down the following day."

With all things sorted Millie managed to get the last train from Liverpool arriving at St Pancras at 1.15am. On the way she was thinking about Jamie and how he would have loved this moment. She wondered if when Jane got out of hospital, she should sit down with her and tell her about Liam's diary and the things he wrote about Cabhan and Shona.

THE HURT OF YOCHANA

The following morning Millie was at the hospital for 9.00am. She rushed to the ward passing the nurses desk and the sight that met could not have been better. Jane was sitting up looking radiant eating her breakfast.

Jane screamed when she saw Millie, "Aunty Millie." They hugged for ages eventually Millie sat on the bed and they started to piece together Jane's missing years.

"Where's uncle Jamie? I thought he would have been sitting by my bed, Aunty Millie." Millie held Jane's hand and calmly told what had happened to her Uncle Jamie. Jane went very quiet and stared at Millie in disbelief.

"I always thought Uncle Jamie would live forever Aunty Millie." A tear rolled down Millie's cheek.

THE HURT OF YOCHANA

"Let me hug you," said Jane. They again embraced each other. Now for the big bombshell she had to tell Millie about Daniel Liam Egan. Danny had said he wanted to come and talk to his mum, but Millie had told him he would have to wait until tomorrow as they were still doing tests. Millie knew it was a little white lie but what if Jane didn't want Danny? Then what, she thought?

"Jane, do you feel up to what I have to tell you, because this is going to change your life?"

"Of course Aunty Millie. I need to know everything to try and rebuild my life and the lost years."

Ok and Millie held Jane's hand.

"You fell into a coma. What I told you about Liverpool and Nebraska do you remember any of it Jane?"

THE HURT OF
YOCHANA

"Yes, I do Aunty Millie. I remember Liverpool vividly and Nebraska. I know I arranged the sale of the old house and Jenny was going to run the coffee shop in Liverpool."

"Well that's all good, but the next thing I tell you prepare yourself for a bit of a shock."

Jane looked at Millie slightly bewildered, she could remember everything. What could possibly be a shock she thought?

"When you fell into a coma the hospital found you were pregnant."

"What, how could I be?" Jane then coloured up.

"Aunty Millie I have only slept with one boy and that was Matt Babbington, who turned out to be a shit, excuse my French."

THE HURT OF
YOCHANA

"Well the hospital successfully kept the baby and you alive, and you have a healthy fourteen year old boy." Jane cried again.

"I'm not sad Aunty Millie. I am overjoyed. Where is he? What did you call him?"

"Me and Uncle Jamie brought him up. Then when Jamie died I brought him up on my own. He knows you are his mum and he has been to see you every week. Jane, he is so excited to see you but I didn't know if you were well enough for all this, so I said he could come in the morning. I have some pictures of him for you to look at."

"What's his name Aunty Millie?"

"We called him Daniel Liam Egan but he tends to get called Danny." Jane took her time looking at the pictures from when he was born to present day. With a deep breath she looked up at Millie.

"He looks so much like Dad, Aunty Millie."

"Uncle Jamie always said that. He has your eyes though. Blimey he is gorgeous, isn't he?" Jane said.

"Yes, and he is a lovely lad too Jane."

"I can't wait to see him Aunty Millie."

"He will be over first thing tomorrow. Jane, it maybe too soon to ask you but have you been dreaming while you were in a coma?"

"Yes, I have Aunty Millie. I remember things so vivid. I will write them in my diary like Dad did." Jane suddenly realised what she had said.

"So you know about your father's diaries then Jane?"

THE HURT OF
YOCHANA

"I'm sorry Aunty Millie, but one time when you and Uncle Jamie had gone away for the weekend I noticed them on the side. I know I should not have looked but once I read the first page I was gripped."

"Why did you never ask us about them Jane?"

"I felt like I had betrayed you. They were given to you not me."

"I wish your Uncle Jamie was alive today he would have been so relieved. We had talked about this day for so many years and all along you knew. We just didn't want to upset you sweetheart," Millie said.

"Well now I have to ask you something. When Dad had his seizures were they like mine?"

"Yes, they were Jane. You appear to have the same condition but also you seem to have the same I suppose you could call it time travel dreaming ability, just like your Dad."

"The dreams don't worry me Aunty Millie. In fact I want to know what happens." Jane started to tell Millie about Yochana and what had happened. Millie could feel a coldness run down her spine. It was the same scenario as Liam, just a different story. Millie just hoped that it all ended ok for Jane.

It was now 8.30pm and the nurse insisted that Millie let Jane get some rest, as they needed to do more tests first thing in the morning.

The nurse led Millie out and she closed the curtains round Jane.

"Doctor Franklin would like a word with you in his office."

THE HURT OF
YOCHANA

Millie was shown into Doctor Franklin's office. The doctor stood up to welcome Millie. He was a tall man, about six foot three inches with thinning brown hair and he had a small wart or something of that nature on his left cheek.

"Do sit down Mrs. Egan. I am Doctor Simon Franklin and I have attended Jane for the last fourteen years, which to my knowledge is possibly the longest time for a coma patient I have attended. The first thing we noticed over the last fourteen years is that Jane's brain was very active, a good sign if we knew why. What I wanted to ask you is has Jane ever mentioned that she used to dream? I think she has what we call Maladaptive Daydreaming or MD for short. People who have this disorder often find days, or weeks even are lost to their dreams. It was not until 2002 a gentleman called Eli Somer PhD came up with this theory. He said that these dreams are most likely caused by trauma or abuse. Can you shed any light on this?"

Millie started to unravel what she knew about Liam Egan and how this seems to have triggered something in his daughter Jane.

"This really helps Mrs. Egan because very little research has been done. We are unsure if this is an imbalance in the brain." Millie sat listening to the doctor knowing he wasn't correct but he was trying to put a tag on it, as some kind of illness.

"Theorists think that this may be a disassociate personality disorder because people with such a personality are detached from their immediate surroundings in both a physical and emotional way. I wish to run tests on Jane now that she is out of a coma. The problem we have is that I can't explain this to her, or her mind I believe will shut down as some kind of defence mechanism. So with your permission, Jane will think we are monitoring her for other reasons."

"How will this help Jane doctor?"

"Well we may be able to find what triggered the attack and then by a process of elimination we could possibly reduce the risk of it happening again."

"Well if it won't harm Jane then we have no choice Doctor Franklin. Her son is coming to see her in the morning."

"Well if you don't mind coming around lunchtime. By then we will have all the wires off Jane and some data to work with."

THE HURT OF
YOCHANA

"Ok Doctor Franklin," said Millie and she left the hospital.

That night the doctor explained to Jane that they needed to do tests while she slept and they gave her a mild sedative. Within ten minutes Jane was back in Yochana's world and the despair and brutality that lived there.

There were hundreds of people lined up in a long shed. There were mainly women. And of course the brutal guards. Yochana and Astera were pushed onto to two sewing machines. Yochana looked at Astera and whispered "I don't know how to use this." Astera put her lips to her mouth for me to be quiet. One of the German guards who we would later call 'Brzydki Czlowiek', the ugly one, came over to Yochana, "What are you saying, Jew whore?" Yochana replied in German

THE HURT OF
YOCHANA

that she had said they looked like good machines. He looked at her with his steely blue eyes, her heart was racing. With her life feeling like it was hanging in the balance he suddenly started laughing and said Yochana should produce a lot of tunics then and he walked away. Over the coming weeks and months Yochana got quite adept with the sewing machine and was often given extra ration of bread, well if you could call it bread, it was always moldy. But she always shared with Astera.

Months had now gone by when both Yochana and Astera were called to the Commandant's office. Herr Schlupp was a portly man, his buttons on his tunic straining to keep his belly concealed. They were told to stand in front of him. Their smelly dresses and dirty hair must not have been a pretty sight, but for some reason he took to Yochana.

"Listen to what I tell you and you will come to no harm. You two are going to work in the gardens, growing vegetables for me and my family. When your day is finished, you will cook the family meal and serve us. Then at some point during the night one of the guards will take you back to your accommodation."

"But I have rules, you only go where you are told, you never steal food or belongings because if you do you will be shot. Do I make myself clear?"

"They both said yes.

"Guard, take these women get them washed, and then set them to work in the garden." The guard saluted the Commandant and they were marched to a shower block. They had heard rumours that they killed people in the shower blocks but they had faith, and why would he say all these things if he was going to kill them? They were given a small bar of soap between them and they cleaned themselves. It felt so good, Yochana could not describe the feeling that she was a woman again. They were in the shower when the guard told them to get out and he threw a dress at each of them. They both thanked him. This took the guard by surprise and he became relaxed. He asked if they wanted a cigarette. They both said they didn't smoke. The guard smiled and told them to sit on the wooden bench.

"My name is Gunther Muller. I am sorry for the brutality you and your people are living through. It is not of my doing."

Gunther began his story he said he was a doctor but had believed all the propaganda put out by the Nazis so he joined the SS. He said his parents and especially his father pleaded with him not to be part of this, as one day the world would want somebody to pay for Hitler's crimes.

"To this day I regret my final words to him. That he was a silly old fool and the Jews cost us the First World War and the Fuhrer would lead our nation to greatness again."

Gunther said he joined up in 1937 and what a mistake he realised he had made. He said he had ended up Bridenbuf in 1940. He said a letter he had sent home to his father apologising for his tirade when he left, and saying that his father was correct was intercepted by the Gestapo. As a punishment he was sent to Bridenbuf. Gunther then started to cry.

THE HURT OF
YOCHANA

"They took my mother and father and tied them to the village monument. Then they poured petrol on them and set them alight. They made me watch from the back of an army truck." Yochana didn't know what to do so she put her arm round him and held him. After a few moments he gathered himself.

"You promise you tell no one." They both promised. Gunther said he would try to look after them. At last they felt they had an ally.

He told us it was August 1941. He took them to the gardens and they set to walk digging and planting. They picked potatoes, marrow, runner beans and turnips. Astera said the turnip tops would make a great side dish instead of lettuce. They collected eggs from the chicken run While they were in there Gunther gave them and apple each. They quickly digested the apple knowing that if another guard saw them it would be certain death for both of them, and possibly Gunther as well. He then took them to the kitchen. On the salt slab was a pig. He said we had to butcher it, then pack it and put it in the ice house at the bottom of the garden. Luckily for Yochana Astera knew how to butcher animals so they set about butchering the pig. They sneakily ate some of the scraps. Gunther just looked the other way. Not all Germans are evil Yochana thought.

Gunther told them that the Commandant and his family, and some selected officers would sit down for dinner at 7.15pm prompt. By the time the meal was finished and they had cleaned up they would be back at the hut by 10.30pm. It was always

THE HURT OF
YOCHANA

6.45am when the sirens woke them to be taken to work.

They chatted as they cut the pig up and prepared dinner. Astera said she knew her mother and father were dead, and two uncles were dead. She said she thought her sister and brother were alive, either in a ghetto or one of the work camps. She said her sister was called Maria and her brother was called Yugis. Yochana told her about her friend Mateusz and how they eventually got caught.

It was at this point that Yochana decided that she would escape if the chance arose and take her chances on the outside. She never told Astera, but from that day every spare moment she would be thinking of an escape plan.

THE HURT OF
YOCHANA

They had a fair life. Gunther became a good friend to Yochana and Astera. The Commandant was impressed with the food they served, and told Gunther once a week they could have a meal. They both smuggled as much as they dare to the others in their hut you could tell just by looking at them that they were fed and the others weren't.

Little was Yochana to know but Christmas Eve 1941 was to be the worse day of her life. Gunther had been allowed to go home for three days over the Christmas period which was Christmas Eve, Christmas day and Boxing Day. The guard who replaced him was Draxler. He was quite a big man who had a reputation with the girls at the factory. He would give them stale bread to have sex with them.

THE HURT OF
YOCHANA

The poor girls were so hungry they didn't care anymore.

It was 11.10 pm. They had made food for thirteen officers and their wives. There was music and dancing, and it was quite loud. Draxler approached Astera and told her to strip. She was shaking and started to cry. He hit her and her mouth was bleeding. He told to lie on the kitchen worktop. He looked at Yochana and smiled, and just said, "Pretty one you are my next Christmas present." I shuddered. He dropped his trousers and this disgusting creature shuffled over to poor Astera. As he got closer something in Yochana snapped. She grabbed the biggest kitchen knife and plunged it into his neck. Blood spurted everywhere as he slumped down. Yochana was quite calm and told Astera to help her pull him into the pantry.

THE HURT OF
YOCHANA

Then they mopped the blood up. All the
time Astera was crying. In the end
Yochana slapped her across the face.

"Listen," she said, "you have to pull
yourself together. We are getting out of
here I have seen a way." Whilst this hadn't
gone to plan as Yochana intended, getting
away on her own, she could not leave
Astera now. Yochana told her to wait
while she nipped into the grand hallway.
On the coat racks were two fur coats. They
would need these if they were to survive.
Yochana quickly grabbed them and
headed back to the kitchen. "Here put this
on," she told her, "now follow me." They
grabbed two loaves freshly baked that
morning. A block of cheese and two
bottles of wine and they ran into the
garden. Behind the potting shed Yochana
had noticed a break in the wire fence.

THE HURT OF
YOCHANA

Although they were outside the camp there were still obstacles to get over. Yochana remembered what Mateusz had told her about going through water because the dogs would not pick up their scent. They stood at the top of a banking that led down to the shallow river below.

"Slide," Yochana said to Astera and they slid down the muddy bank until they reached the river.

"Walk in the water Astera, until sunrise then we will know which is east." They waded down the river for about 3 hours so they assumed they had done about nine miles. At a clearing they sat and ate the bread and cheese, and drank one of the wines. Well it is Christmas they thought.

They both fell asleep.

Back at the hospital Jane was surrounded by doctors and nurses, she appeared to be having another seizure. The doctors had phoned Millie and she was outside with Danny. It was pandemonium around Jane's bed as the doctors battled with the poor girl. Eventually it all calmed down and Dr. Franklin came out and gestured for Millie and Danny to follow him to his office.

"I am afraid this is not good news. We monitored Jane during the night and at 2.00am she asked a nurse for a pen and paper. She appears to be dreaming but has documented everything," and Franklin pushed the paper at Millie.

"This is dreadful doctor, she is living the life of Yochana."

"When she finished writing, because I am monitoring her she fell straight back into a deep sleep and her brain became

over active again. Whilst I was monitoring
her I looked up the name Yochana. It
means thoughtful and in some instances it
is a Jewish name meaning Jane!"

"What happens now?"

"All we can do is monitor her until the
next seizure. Hopefully by then I will have
data to try and correct what is happening. I
have a colleague coming up from Oxford,
he has done a lot of research on the brain
and the mind, and more importantly
dreams and regression. He should be here
later today. Once I have briefed him on
Jane you can talk to him." Franklin
showed them out of his office.

"I believe the cafeteria is open for
breakfast if you are hungry."

"Thank you doctor," said Millie, and
Danny and Millie went to the cafeteria.
Neither could eat and so Millie got two

THE HURT OF
YOCHANA

coffees and decided to tell Danny everything because the poor lad could have the same problems in the future.

Danny seemed shocked when Millie opened up about his granddad and his Mum.

"We didn't want to hold it from you, but this is some kind of illness that was passed from father to daughter and it may have been passed onto you Danny."

Danny said he had a million questions but didn't know where to start.

Meanwhile in Yochana's world they were awakened by sirens in the distance. Although they thought they must have walked about nine miles, they could see in the distance search light lighting up the dawn sky. Astera asked if they were going to be ok.

THE HURT OF YOCHANA

"I don't think they will find us. There are no tracks to pick up from the river bed and no scent for the dogs. They cuddled together to keep warm their fur coats a welcome feel on the wretched bodies. They sat for a while, and then made their way along a road with a small road sign pointing to Dimlumb. The roads and surrounding countryside appeared flat. She dare not say this Astera, but Yochana thought they were in Holland. What the girls didn't know was Holland was occupied by now. Astera was quite a timid girl, easily upset whereas Yochana had become harden by all she had experienced.

"Astera, we need to find food and that is best done at night. This town appears very quiet so we should hide here until dusk then go and find food." The girls had found a garden shed on an allotment so they hid there. They had been there about an hour when it suddenly dawned on Yochana.

"Astera, we haven't seen a single person anywhere yet."

"What do you mean?" Astera said.

"Well everything seems deserted to me." It was soon dusk again and the girls decided to take their chances but everywhere was deserted, there were no soldiers and no people. They stumbled across a small low roofed house and made their way down the side. The house appeared deserted so Yochana smashed the glass in the door not thinking that the door would not be open anyway but it was! The house was empty but there were packets of dried egg and quite a few packets of something called Stamppot, which looked like dried stew. Astera looked in the larder, "Quick," she said, "there is a half of pig." The girls were that hungry they tucked into the raw meat of the pig. It smelt a bit but that didn't matter it was food, they thought. As soon as they had their fill they started looking round the house. It had three bedrooms, and whatever happened, all the beds had been made and it was very tidy. The girls lay on the twin beds and were soon asleep.

Back in London Jane was still in a coma the doctors had called Millie and Danny in twice. They were totally baffled by her condition. Doctor Franklin, who was the senior doctor, had now taken on the responsibility of Jane's welfare. He told Millie that Jane did not appear to be stressed, but there was an awful lot of brain activity. A lot more he said than what he would have expected from a person in Jane's position.

"This is baffling all of us, Mrs. Trench, we really are at a loss. All we can do is wait and hope Jane comes out of this." Although Millie was upset she had to be strong for Danny. She nodded her head and Doctor Franklin said he would keep them both posted on any improvements.

Millie and Danny hardly spoke on the way home. Millie decided that she should tell Danny about his granddad Liam and the dreams and the diary, and then explain about his mum. Millie had felt guilty for some years about Jane and the fact that Jamie had Liam's diary.

When they got home she made Danny a cup of coffee and they sat by the fire and Millie started to explain about Cabhan and Shona and Liam. Danny sat listening. He

asked a few questions, but he was
basically finding it hard to take in. Millie
thought it was time to produce the diary.
Danny sat cross legged by the roaring fire
and read and read. Millie was pottering
about doing little jobs round the house.
Two hours passed when Millie saw Danny
close the diaries.

"Do you understand a bit more now
Danny?"

"I'm not sure Aunty Millie," he said. It
was now or never Millie thought so she
produced Jane's diary. Danny again sat
crossed leg not saying a word for an hour
and a half then he closed the diary looked
at Millie and said, "Mum is going to die
isn't she Aunty Millie?"

"I don't know that Danny."

"Will this curse be in me Aunty Millie?"

THE HURT OF YOCHANA

"Probably not. I would not worry about it; your Mum will come around again. She has just had a relapse, let's try and be positive." All the time Millie was saying the words she felt sick to the pit of her stomach. Maybe Jane would not survive and maybe Danny did carry the curse as he put it. Oh how she wished Jamie was still alive.

Millie was finding it very hard to keep her emotions in check. She needed to be strong for poor Danny who had thought at last he had got his Mum back, only to find she was taken from him again.

The next day, Danny and Jane made their way to the hospital. Doctor Franklin had just finished his rounds so he took them in his office.

"I have some good news and just a small amount of bad news. Well possibly not bad news, but something we can't understand."

Franklin said that tests he was running were showing Jane was calm although he wasn't sure if this was good or bad for her. He said Jane's brain seemed to be very active and he had never seen this in a patient in Jane's condition before. Jane also spoke to one of the nurses last night. Again this is most unusual

"We actually thought she was coming out of the coma but it was a false dawn."

"What did she say Doctor Franklin?"

"She just said Astera. Does that mean anything to you?" Millie decided to fill in Doctor Franklin on the diaries and Liam's condition. He was aware, but Millie went into the situation much deeper.

"Could I read the diaries Mrs. Trench?"

THE HURT OF
YOCHANA

"I don't see why not if you think it may help the situation."

"Well I can't promise anything but you never know. It certainly can't harm anything and it may help me understand the brain pattern reading I am getting from monitoring Jane." Luckily Danny had brought them with him as he said he was going to talk to his Mum about the diaries.

"That would have been a very good idea young man," said Doctor Franklin. "I will only need them for a day, and then I will give them back to you." Danny passed Doctor Franklin the diaries and they proceeded to Jane's bedside.

Jane's dreams were on-going, although nobody in the real world could know the horrors the poor girl was going through in her nightmare state.

THE HURT OF
YOCHANA

Yochana and Astera woke from their sleep almost together. There was an eerie silence in the house. They crept to the bedroom window and peered outside. There was absolutely nobody on the street, no civilians and no soldiers. What had they stumbled on in this town?

"This is so weird Astera, why would a whole town just disappear?" Astera shrugged her shoulders, she was a lady of very few words.

"Come on Astera, we best see if there are any clothes we can wear to keep us warm." In the first bedroom the walls were painted lilac, it was very pretty Yochana thought. On the dressing table was a picture of a family. There was a lady, a gentleman, two young children and what appeared to be two sets of grandparents. Everything was neat and tidy as if they had just left that day. Astera started looking through the oak chest of draws which was adorned by a big picture mirror.

"Look Yochana, gloves," she cried in pure excitement she also found a matching sheepskin hat to wear. In the wardrobe Yochana had found several coats, all very good quality. Whoever lived here was certainly wealthy she thought. In one of the pockets she found an identity card with a name Pieje Oomen.

"What happened here Yochana?"

"My guess would be they were rounded up by the Germans and sent to work camps. But what I don't understand is why all the clothes and possessions were not taken by whoever moved these people on. They changed their clothes and by now Yochana had also found a warm hat and gloves and they decided to take a look round this ghost town. They left by the back kitchen nervously walked down the side of the house which fronted onto the road. Everything seemed different from when they arrived in the dead of night. They kept to the alleyways but all the shops were empty; the bakers, the ironmongers, butchers, a lady's dress shop and a bicycle shop. It was just like the villagers just decided one day to leave and never return, but took nothing with them. The town of Dimlumb was a ghost town, or so they thought. They scurried down an alleyway and watched as two open top cars with Gestapo staff pulled up with seven canvas covered lorries behind them. Yochana understood the German general talking and barking orders.

THE HURT OF
YOCHANA

"Do you understand what they say Yochana?" said Astera.

"Yes, he is telling them to build a fortified fence round the village as the Jews will be brought here to work before transporting to the death camps.

"Shush Astera, let me listen," said Yochana. He said the villagers were forced out by the Gestapo and marched to Germany as prisoners of war.

"Wow, now what do we do Yochana?"

"Well let's go back to the house and try and eat what there is. Then we need to get out of this village by nightfall before they start putting the fencing up and we are trapped here."

The girls headed back to the house and ate more of the raw pig and some stale cake that they found. They filled three bottles with water and put them with some

more pig and cake into a rucksack they
had found. Then sat and waited until
2.00am, which Mateusz had said was
always the best time to move as the
soldiers on duty were often asleep.

With everything ready and a full moon
in the sky the girls headed out of Dimlumb
with all their hopes of one day finding
freedom.

Down the small alley the girls scurried
like rats. After about a mile they could see
a sign which said welcome to Dimlumb so
they knew they were on the outskirts of
the village.

"Where are we going Yochana?" Astera
asked in a timid voice.

"Look up to the stars, can you see that
one? That's the North Star from that I can
get us to the coast then hopefully to
Britain. My father taught me a little about

astronomy and how the sailors guided their boats. Come on Astera follow me it's our only hope."

The girls only walked at night and some nights the sky was too hazy to see the stars. On the way they ate berries to stay alive and drank from village fountains when they could, although this was risky. They assumed they were walking about twenty miles each night before it was too light, so they would then go into hiding. Astera had marked on her arm each day and at thirty days they could hear seagulls. There had been many close shaves on the way but now they could see a small town in the distance. Although weak from the lack of food and water, and their feet swollen and bruised, they felt finally they may taste freedom.

THE HURT OF
YOCHANA

After resting, they set off for one final push. Magadha was the name on the village sign and on the town hall they could see a small Union Jack. With the pain in their feet they walked down the cobbled street to the town hall. The shout went up "Who goes their friend or foe?" They could hardly talk, they were that weak. Two British Tommie's put down their rifles and helped them into the town hall.

"Get the nurse and doctor," one of the soldiers said. By now both Astera and Yochana had fainted. When they came round, they were in a small hospital.

"Where are we?" said Yochana to one of the nurses.

"You are in Holland my dear," said the kindly grey haired British nurse.

THE HURT OF YOCHANA

"You are both safe now my dear. Now let's see what we can rustle up for your breakfast." The girls were in beds side by side, and either side of them were what must have been a wounded soldier and a lady. Next to Astera the soldier had a bandage covering his head and one eye and he only had one leg. To the side of Yochana was a lady, she had had a bullet would in her arm.

"So where have you two come from?" the lady asked Yochana. Yochana started telling her story. The lady seemed intrigued. Astera although shy was talking to the wounded soldier.

After a couple of weeks of recuperation, the girls were now strong enough to try and get to Great Britain. Yochana had struck up quite a friendship with the lady who said her name was Esta Lincoln. Esta

THE HURT OF
YOCHANA

told Yochana she was a British spy. Her job was to get into towns and ghettos, and relay information back to the soldiers on numbers of civilians and soldiers and how the civilians were being treated. Esta spoke very good German, Dutch and English so Yochana could see how this could be plausible.

"We have watched you Yochana and I want you to join us."

"What about Astera?"

"I am afraid Astera would not be able to carry it off. You on the other hand, could help the fight against these bastards. Surely you want to do this Yochana?" Esta said.

"I have no hesitation Esta, but I need to get my friend to safety."

THE HURT OF
YOCHANA

"Don't worry about Astera we will get her to England."

"Do you promise Esta?"

"I give you my word."

"Then I will join you. When do we start?"

"Tomorrow, we are going to work in a café in Glugon near Paris. The underground runs it. Our cover is we are German and we work there."

"Can you tell I am a Polish Jew Esta?"

"No you can't, you are beautiful, the German soldiers won't be able to take their eyes of you. They will never think for one minute you are Jewish.

"I will keep my name, but we should call you a German name, what would you like?"

"I had a friend at school that was called Anina and I always liked that name."

THE HURT OF
YOCHANA

"Ok Anina it is then. Now go and spend the night with your friend before she leaves for England."

"I will meet you here at 9.00am tomorrow morning Yochana or should I say Anina," and she smiled.

Yochana sat with Astera and told her of her decision.

"You are so brave Yochana, I wish I was like you."

"Astera you have done so well. We have got you freedom never forget that."

"Oh, I won't Yochana and I will never forget you." The two girls snuggled down for the night.

At 6.30pm they were woken by a man called Michael who was to take Astera to England.

"Here," said Astera and she handed Yochana a lock of hair. Yochana also had nothing, but she cut a lock of hair and gave it to Astera.

"When the war is over I will look for you my friend. Let's keep the locks of hair safe."

"Good luck my friend and thank you for everything," and Astera hugged Yochana. With tears rolling down both young girl's faces they parted waving. As she went Astera thought this would be the last time she may see her friend the brave Yochana.

Back in the hospital Millie had gone for two coffees. Danny was playing on his phone when suddenly Jane woke just as Millie arrived with the coffees. Jane looked at Millie then Danny.

"Are you my son?" Danny stood up. He was like his granddad, quite tall. He put his arms round Jane and hugged her. They were crying with joy and Millie was crying from relief that Jane seemed ok.

By the time a nurse had heard the commotion Jane was sat up talking as if nothing had happened. The nurse called another nurse to fetch Doctor Franklin. Franklin could not believe his eyes. How Jane looked and was talking, he wanted to hug everyone but his professional persona won.

Two days passed and Millie got a call from Doctor Franklin.

"Doctor Franklin is everything ok?"

"Absolutely my dear. Jane is well enough to go home today. If you would come just after lunch she will be ok to leave."

Millie phoned Danny's school and they said he could go with Millie to get his

THE HURT OF
YOCHANA

Mum. When they arrived Jane was waiting. She looked radiant.

"You look so well Jane."

"Thank you Aunty Millie, and look at my big boy," and she hugged Danny.

"The doctor would like to see you all before you go please," and the nurse showed them into Doctor Franklin's office.

"Well Jane," he said, "you are a bit of a medical phenomenon," and he smiled.

"I have been involved with the study of the brain for more years than I care to remember, and I have never seen anything so incredible in my life. I have spent many hours with colleagues looking for answers. I have to tell you we don't have any. The only factor I think may cause your problem is stress, but I cannot be certain of that because when you are in a coma

THE HURT OF
YOCHANA

your brain is very active but you are relaxed. Again, I don't have a clue, it goes against all known medical science. I hope, and please don't take this the wrong way, that we never see you again because then I will know you are ok. Go and enjoy your son and your life Jane." Jane couldn't help herself she pecked Doctor Franklin on the cheek.

Millie insisted Jane came and stayed with her and Danny for six months without saying it she needed to be sure she wouldn't have any more relapses. They arrived at Millie's place and Millie started cooking lunch. Jane and Danny sat getting to know each other and Danny was showing all the pictures Millie and Jamie had taken.

It was almost 10.30 pm when Jane said she was a bit tired but asked Millie for her diary as she wanted to write down what else had happened, her dreams appeared to be in months where her real life had been moving on in years. Millie wasn't sure about the diaries but they were Jane's so she handed them over. Jane retired to her bedroom and set about writing all the details of Yochana's life down in the diary from her dreams. Jane noticed that Millie had kept the rose and the vase that Maria Klinck had given her all those years before. What was the significance she thought as she hurriedly wrote down the content of the dreams?

Jane finished as far as her dreams had taken her and flopped back on the bed and fell fast asleep.

Now her dreams took over again and she was standing with Esta dressed as a waitress in the German restaurant. How

THE HURT OF
YOCHANA

she hated the German officers with their
arrogance, smoking cigars and quaffing
the most expensive whisky. Every now
and again as she waited on the tables one
of them would get amorous with her and
she would have to smile then giggle as if it
was ok to paw her. When she told Esta
about these disgusting men, Esta simply
replied, "We are here to get information.
Think of all those poor people in those
camps praying every night for this
dreadful war to end and if we can make
that happen sooner, think how many lives
we could save."

"I know Esta, just they disgust me."

"They disgust me Yochana, sorry I must
make sure I get into the habit of calling
you Anina, or that slip of the tongue could
be the difference between life and death."
Anina nodded in agreement. At the end of

the shift the girls cleaned up. There was one officer left who had taken a shine to Anina. As she went past his table and he grabbed her.

"What is your name?" he said in a strong German accent. She very nearly said Yochana but corrected herself.

"My name is Anina."

"Well Anina you are very pretty. Let's get some wine and I am sure we could have a room for the night." Anina felt sick to the pit of her stomach but she knew she had to do this.

"You woman," he said pointing to Esta, "get me wine and a room for me and this lovely girl." Esta got two bottles of wine and two glasses and gave them a key to room number three on the second landing.

THE HURT OF
YOCHANA

"You can go now," he said to Esta. "Me
and Anina are going to have some fun,
aren't we pretty lady?"

"Go with Sturmbannfuhrer Sechen to
room number three Anina." He grabbed
Anina by the arm and in his drunken state
made her climb the stairs with him to
bedroom number three. All the time he
was touching her she wanted to throw up.
Inside the bedroom her instructions were
to sleep with him, but try and find out
where the next ghetto was to be emptied
and the people taken to the death camps.

This man was an animal he pulled at her
clothes laughing. He stank of stale cigars
and brandy. He fell over twice trying to
take his trousers off. By now Anina was
only partial dressed. He ordered her onto
the bed, and then the big ugly fat pig tried
to have sex with her. She couldn't bear it

anymore and by instinct she grabbed the candle holder and hit him on the head. He dropped onto her almost suffocating her. Anina managed to squirm from under him but she knew instantly that she had killed him. Hearing the noise, Esta came rushing in.

"What have you done Yochana?"

"I couldn't do it Esta. It was horrible," Yochana was shaking and crying. Esta called one of the chefs.

"We have to dispose of his body where nobody will find him Gunther," she said. Gunther looked frightened.

"We need to gather our thoughts here Esta." Esta looked at Yochana. She said, "You need to go. You are on your own, if this gets out all our lives will be in danger. I will give you some money try and head back."

THE HURT OF
YOCHANA

"I thought you could do this Yochana."
Yochana started to cry, "I am so sorry
Esta."

"Go now and we will dispose of his
body. When they come looking they may
think both have run off together."

Yochana left the café and with a tatty
map, some sandwiches and a drink. She
set off back to Magadha and hopefully
freedom in Britain.

Only travelling at night, it took twelve
days to finally see Magadha town hall in
the distance. By now Yochana's feet were
swollen cut and bruised. She had eaten
berries on the way and drank water from
streams but she wasn't in a good way
when she finally landed at the make shift
hospital. Everyone remembered her.

THE HURT OF
YOCHANA

Typical of Yochana, although she was so ill her only concern was had Astera got to Britain safely. Yochana spent three weeks recovering with the Red Cross nurses. One morning a tall dark haired, quite handsome chap called Captain William Nichol approached Yochana. He introduced himself but first he removed his brown leather gloves. He explained that he was in charge of getting people to Britain and relative safety. He told Yochana that it was decision time. She could if she wished stay and help at the make–shift hospital or leave the following night for Britain. He stated that both options had risks and he would need an answer in the morning. But before he left Yochana, he gave her a book that Astera had left behind for her friend should she ever return he said. The book was called

THE HURT OF
YOCHANA

'Broken promises are for broken people.' Yochana though it strange but thanked the Captain telling him she would give him an answer in the morning. Yochana left the kitchen area where the meeting had taken place, and headed for the dormitory she had been allocated which housed four people. Yochana sat on the bed and opened the book. Inside the book was a white envelope and inside was a pressed rose flower.

Yochana settled down with the book. She could not put the book down, she read and read. It was if the book had been written about her. She managed to get to the end or at least to the last page which was page number 242 the rest of the pages were missing.

THE HURT OF YOCHANA

Jane suddenly woke up sweating. Millie and Danny were stood over her.

"Are you ok Jane?"

"Oh Aunty Millie, there is so much happening in these dreams and now they appear to be mirroring my life here."

"What do you mean Jane?" Jane explained about the rose and the book 'Broken promises are for broken people.'

"The book is about a girl from when she was born to when she was thirty seven."

"What happened then?"

"All the pages had gone so I don't know Aunty Millie."

"Danny nip and get your mum a cup of tea please." Once Danny was out of ear shot Millie asked Jane how she was.

"I'm frightened Aunty Millie, do the missing pages mean I am going to die?"

THE HURT OF
YOCHANA

"No sweetheart, but maybe we should seek some help. Your dad went to see Nicola Gielbert who is a regression specialist. She was very good with Liam, we could see if that could help."

"Do you think it might?"

"I don't honestly know Jane, but we don't want you fretting or it may bring on your illness again, so it's probably worth a shot."

"Ok Aunty Millie." Danny brought his mum the tea and Jane managed to put a brave face on things for Danny's sake.

"Let's go shopping and have mother and son time."

"What a great idea Jane," Millie said.

While Jane and Danny were off shopping Millie phoned Nicola Gielbert and explained the situation. At first Nicola Gielbert seemed distant as if she didn't

THE HURT OF
YOCHANA

want to know. Millie pleaded with her so she agreed to just meet Millie that afternoon to discuss if she could be of any help. They agreed to meet at a Maria's Tea House in Covent Garden at 1.30pm that afternoon.

The tea house was very popular with the tourists in Covent Garden due to all the waitresses wearing Victorian clothing. Luckily they managed to find seats in the window.

"So Mrs. Trench what is the problem?"

"Jane Egan is Liam Egan's daughter who you treated with regression."

"Oh Mr. Egan yes, I remember now. He was a nice man but I had never seen such intense regression then or since. How is he?"

"I am afraid he passed away."

"Oh, I am sorry."

THE HURT OF
YOCHANA

"It isn't Liam I have come to discuss. It's his daughter Jane, she is living the same nightmare it appears."

"Please explain more clearly," Nicola Gielbert said in her husky French accent. Millie started to tell Nicola Gielbert everything that had happened to Jane since she moved to Liverpool for University. The whole story took over an hour and three coffees to complete to present day. All the time Nicola Gielbert listened intensely.

"Mrs. Trench I have spoken to many fellow professionals about Liam Egan, confidentially of course. He appears to be the only patient to have ever had such a dramatic dream or regression pattern as we would call it. I am unsure if I helped or hindered Mr. Egan and I would not want to in anyway give false hope to his daughter, Mrs. Trench."

"I understand Nicola, but she is frightened. She thinks she is going to die. If we could just find out what the significance of the rose meant."

"Ok, maybe that would be a starting point Mrs. Trench. I will see Jane tomorrow at my premises at 2.30pm. Does that work for you?"

"Thank you, Nicola."

"We will concentrate on the rose then see what happens. Goodbye Mrs. Trench. I will see you tomorrow." Nicola Gielbert made her excuses and left. Millie watched her walking into the crowd in Covent Garden thinking how stylish she looked in her white dress, mink coat and Christian Leboutin brown high heels. She looked assured and very self-confident as she strode from the tea room and disappeared into the mass of tourists of every nationality. Millie finished her coffee and called Jane and told her about the meeting and the need to get to the bottom of the rose, and then maybe they could piece together the story. Millie, who had always been level headed, wondered if they could piece the story together it would then stop the dreams and Jane could have a normal life. Well that is what she was hoping for!

When Millie arrived home Jane and Danny were looking at Jane's diary. She could see a strange bond developing between Jane and Danny, not just a mother son bond but also a common thread. Millie wondered if she should speak with Jane, or if all those years ago, the decision Jamie and she took had created today's situation with the dreams. Was Danny about to be another victim of this awful affliction?

"Hi you two," she said in her cheeriest voice.

"Hi Aunty Millie," they replied but were so engrossed in the diary they hardly looked up.

"What would you both like for tea?"

"Can I nip to the chip shop for us Aunty Millie?" Danny said.

"Fine by me, what about you Jane?"

"Sorry Aunty Millie I am miles away."

"Yes, Fish and Chips would be nice." Millie gave Danny twenty pounds as he was leaving. This was her chance to tell Jane about the meeting with Nicola Gielbert and her appointment tomorrow.

"Jane I need to talk to you."

"What's the matter Aunty Millie?" Millie proceeded to tell Jane of her meeting and what she thought it would achieve if she went to the appointment the following day. At first Jane seemed apprehensive but then looked at Millie.

"Aunty Millie I will never know how to repay you for what you have done for me. Bringing Danny up, visiting me and caring for me through the dark times. You are a very special person and both me and Danny love you to the end of the world and back. If you think this could help me of course I will go. Do you think we should tell Danny?"

"I am glad you brought that up Jane. I'm not sure sharing your dreams is good for him. I am frightened it may trigger something in his sub-conscious. What you have gone through and your father and mother are beyond words. I am hoping this thing ends and Danny isn't affected."

THE HURT OF
YOCHANA

"Guess you are saying no to telling him then. You are so wise Aunty Millie, you know I would not hurt Danny I just never thought. The dream thing is weird I miss it but don't want to be poorly. It's a bit like waiting for your next fix of a TV soap." Just then Danny arrived back.

"You lay the table Danny," said Millie. "I will butter the bread and you make a drink Jane." They sat eating at the table and Millie thought how well Jane looked. Hopefully tomorrow might get to the bottom of the rose and the dreams.

Mum don't forget I am away from tomorrow on the school skiing trip to Switzerland.

"I know Danny, everything is sorted. You said your mate's dad was picking you up."

"Yes Mr. Barton."

THE HURT OF
YOCHANA

"Well you perhaps should have an early night," and Jane kissed Danny.

Jane and Millie sat talking into the early hours of the morning but the subject always came back to the dreams. It was 1.30am when Jane and Millie finally went to bed. Because they had discussed the dreams Jane thought she would be dreaming and back in Yochana's world. But she didn't. She woke up at 9.00am when Danny came into her room all excited.

"See you mum I will phone you."

"You better son," and they embraced. Danny left excited, waving as he left with his multi-coloured bobble hat that Millie had knitted perched precariously on his head.

THE HURT OF YOCHANA

Millie and Jane decided to do a bit of shopping before heading for Nicola Gielbert's practice.

"Don't want to ask you Jane, but I must. Did you dream last night?"

"No Aunty Millie, nothing, in fact I had a wonderful night's sleep.

"Oh well, let's hope we can get closure today for you sweetheart." After a couple of coffees and the purchasing of a few dresses and some shoes they arrived at Gielbert's office.

The offices hadn't changed much and memories of Liam came flooding back. Nicola Gielbert was her usual confident self, dressed in brown leather trousers and a cream blouse with a small silver cross necklace sitting seductively near her bosom. She wore a pair of cream Jimmy Choo kitten heels. Millie knew what they were, she was a shoe addict. Jamie always said she had more shoes than Imelda Marcos!!

"Hello Jane nice to meet you. What we are going to do today is that I will transgress you, and we will try and see what is triggering these dreams of a former life. Before I do this I must tell you there is an element of danger and for that reason you will have to sign this form giving me permission to carry out the regression and to show you fully understand any risks involved."

Jane read the form which was quite involved and after ten minutes she signed the form.

"Your Aunty Millie can hold your hand if you wish. You will hear some calming music. I wish you to lie back on the bed and just relax try and empty all your thoughts. Just think you are floating on a cloud with not a care in the world." After a few minutes Jane appeared asleep.

"Yochana what are you doing?" Gielbert said. Jane said nothing.

"Where are you Yochana?" Jane suddenly spoke but she had a Polish accent.

"I am helping at the hospital."

"Where is the hospital Yochana?" Millie could feel Jane gripping her hand so tight her nails were digging to her skin.

"I'm in Magadha. Why are you asking me these questions am I in trouble?"

"No Yochana. I want to know about the rose."

THE HURT OF
YOCHANA

"The rose I picked in the garden when I was with my Mother and Father or the rose Astera gave me?"

"Tell me about the rose Astera gave you."

"I helped Astera escape the work camp and I managed to get her to Britain. Have you seen her?" Nicola Gielbert paused before answering. Yochana asked again, "have you seen her?" Nicola Gielbert leaned forward and whispered in Millie's ear. "I am going to lie. I need Yochana to think I have seen Astera. This could be what is troubling her." Millie nodded in agreement.

"Yochana, Astera is safe in England. Why did she give you a rose?" Yochana sounded elated and in broken English she said, "A rose represents freedom from the tyrannical Nazis. Astera gave me a book and a pressed rose inside it."

"Millie I think I should bring her out of regression now. Jane I want you to come back to me." There was no sign of Jane hearing. Gielbert tried again. Suddenly Jane spoke as Yochana again, "Are you a spy are you trying to trick me again. I will kill you. I have killed before," she said. Suddenly then Jane woke from the regression.

"Just sit a minute Jane, and we will have a coffee. How are you feeling?"

"I feel fine, did I fall asleep?"

"Just let me make the coffee and I will discuss my findings." Millie was holding Jane's hand. Nicola came back with the coffees.

"Right Jane I feel that was a good first session. I cut it a little short because your regression ego, Yochana was getting a little uptight with the questions and I needed to talk about the rose. Yochana thinks I know that Astera is in Great Britain and safe. This isn't what I would normally do, but I need to gain her confidence. Are there any parts of the regression you can remember Jane?"

"Nothing absolutely nothing."

"Well that is a great sign. I am pleased with the start we have made. Can you come back in a couple of days and we will try a little harder? Do you have your diary with you?"

"Yes, I carry it everywhere."

"May I borrow it until the next session?" Jane was hesitant but finally agreed.

"Well I will see you both in two days' time," and Nicola showed them out.

THE HURT OF
YOCHANA

"She seems a nice lady Aunty Millie."

"Yes she is, and she seemed very assured that she can sort this."

"Part me wants a normal life and part of me feels for Yochana."

"Well we now know the significance of the rose and why Maria Klinck gave it to you that day in Liverpool all those years ago Jane."

"Come on, let's have a drink in Covent Garden and relax we don't have to rush back for Danny."

"That would be lovely Aunty Millie." The girls sat in Ursula's Emporium coffee shop watching the world go by.

"Jane I have to ask you this what are your plans for Ringo's café in Liverpool?"

"Aunty Millie, I have thought about this. With what mum and dad left me, the house I sold in Nebraska, and other things

THE HURT OF YOCHANA

Maria Klinck and her son left me, I think I am going to give the café to Jenny. She deserves it, she has a family now and she has run the business. I think it's only fair. In fact I texted her this morning to see if I could go up this weekend to stay. She hasn't replied yet."

'Ding, ding' Jane's phone lit up.

"Well how flippin' odd she just texted back look. "Of course, so excited to see you. Let me know what time and I will meet you at the train station, love Jenny"

"That is lovely of you Jane. Jenny has been a true friend to you. I think she will be blown away when you tell her."

"I love her like a sister Aunty Millie, so I hope so." It was 10.00pm and copious amounts of Chablis had been drunk when they called a taxi. Back home Millie made them both a milky coffee with a Bailey's

THE HURT OF
YOCHANA

Irish Cream added and they slipped off to bed.

The following morning Millie was up first. she sat watching the news when Jane came through.

"Hello sweetheart did you sleep ok?"

"Yes fine Aunty Millie."

"No dream's?"

"No nothing."

"Oh, I am pleased. What shall we do today?"

"Shall we go to the Tate Gallery, it's years since I have been."

"Yes, why not."

"I am going to call my solicitor to make up the paperwork to transfer the ownership of Ringo's to Jenny. Then we can pick it up tomorrow when we go back to Nicola Gielbert's surgery."

THE HURT OF
YOCHANA

"Good thinking Jane. Well wrap up because it's cold outside." Millie was getting dressed when she looked on the dressing table at a picture of Jamie clowning about on holiday in Indonesia. She smiled to herself, how proud he would have been of Jane she thought.

"Come on Aunty Millie the taxi is here." They arrived at the Tate.

"What a relaxing place Aunty Millie and the David Hockney paintings are incredible."

"I agree."

"Shall we have dinner here? My treat Aunty Millie."

"Ok sweetheart."

"The Rex Whistler restaurant opened up in 1927," Millie said.

"Wow these walls must have some stories to tell."

THE HURT OF
YOCHANA

"You bet Jane." The waiter arrived.

"My name is Gordon, at your service," he said. "Would you like a drink while you choose your meal?" and he offered the wine menu with the food menu.

"Our wine cellar is considered to be one of the finest in Europe, so I am sure you will be able to enjoy something from it."

"Jane, do you mind if we have a bottle of the Domaine Terre Brune? It was Uncle Jamie's favourite. He brought me here for my thirtieth birthday and that's what he ordered."

"Yes, let's go for that please." The waiter left to get the bottle of wine while Jane and Millie decided on their meal. He returned, served the wine and the girls ordered, Jane first.

"I will have Whipped Goats Cheese with Honeycomb Figs, Sorrel and Mustard dressing. And for the main course Chalk Stream Hampshire Trout, new potatoes and pea puree please."

"That sounds nice Jane, I will have something different then we can try each other's." Millie s looked at the waiter who was patiently waiting to take the order. "Sorry but there is so much choice."

"This is not a problem take your time."

"To start I will have the Dumplings, Mayonnaise, Cucumber, Herbs and lemon Capers please, and for my main Tart Tatin with beetroot puree and stilton crumbles on a garlic mash please." The waiter took back the menus and left Jane and Millie chatting.

"This wine is lovely Aunty Millie, Uncle Jamie had good taste."

"Not sure about that Jane," and Millie laughed. "I remember one time me and

THE HURT OF
YOCHANA

Jamie and your mum and dad went to a New Year's Eve party and it was a 70s dressed theme. Your mum went as Sinitta who was beautiful just like your mum. Liam went as Noddy Holder from Slade. I went as Farrah Fawcett Majors with a big blonde wig."

"What was Uncle Jamie, something Italian I bet?"

"Well we had all shared what we were going as but Jamie wouldn't say, so we expected the white suit as John Travolta."

"So, what was he?" by now Jane was crying with laughter as the waiter came with the starters.

"He came.." and then Millie paused because she couldn't stop laughing.

"He came as a Rubik's cube." They were a couple of minutes before the laughter died down then Millie said, "It gets worse, he was trying to show off his dance moves, you know how he liked to dance. Well he fell over because of the cube, he couldn't help himself. He hit his nose on a chair and we had to go accident and emergency. The nurse would not believe he hadn't been fighting as he had broken it in two places." They both laughed again.

"I do miss him Aunty Millie."

"I miss him too Jane, he was the only one for me."

With starter and the main course finished the waiter returned with the sweet menu.

"Can we have another bottle of the wine please?"

"Certainly madam, I will leave you the dessert menu."

"What are you going to have Jane?"

THE HURT OF
YOCHANA

"I don't know, what about you?"

"Oh, look they've got decadent chocolate Frosty cake. Remember when you used to make something like that Aunty Millie?"

"Yes, think I called mine Millie's decadence," and she laughed. Jane ordered it and Millie ordered the Riddle me Ree Lime Chambord tart. It was almost 5.00pm when the girls left, a little tipsy and definitely full of food. Jane put her arm inside Millie's as they walked for a taxi.

"Thank you for everything you have done for me Aunty Millie I love you soooo much." Millie smiled but felt a warm glow inside her Jane may not be her biological daughter but she was certainly her daughter in all other ways she thought.

THE HURT OF YOCHANA

The girls arrived back at Millie's and sat until 9.30pm talking and laughing. Millie was so pleased that Jane seemed to have turned the corner.

"Right Aunty Millie, I am going to get some sleep ready for Nicola Gielbert tomorrow."

"Ok honey, I will finish this and I am going to bed too."

Millie sat looking at a picture of Jamie and Liam together on a golfing trip they had in the Algarve. Liam looking immaculate as always in his golfing attire. Then next to him Jamie with a knotted handkerchief on his head playing the 'Brit Abroad 'and falling about laughing. She felt sadness that she had lost the only man she ever loved but joyful that she had Jane and Danny.

THE HURT OF
YOCHANA

By now Jane was asleep and the dreams started again. It was morning in the make-shift hospital in Magadha and Yochana had to make a decision. She did not know the decision was about to be taken from her. The make-shift hospital was not a nice place to be. The men and women with serious injuries were often crying with pain. Some emergency procedures were carried out without proper equipment or anything to help with the pain, and the screaming coming from the operating theatre was excruciating. Yochana had made her decision to stay so decided to go to Captain Nichol's office. she knocked on the old oak door and a grouchy voice said, "come in."

Nichol was sitting at his desk smoking his pipe and looking at a piece of paper.

THE HURT OF
YOCHANA

"How can I help you my dear?" he said in a real English gentleman's voice.

"I have decided to stay and help you Captain Nichol." He looked at Yochana over the paper he had been looking at.

"I wish I could say that is fine, but I have just had intelligence reports that the Germans are only five miles from us and we are to evacuate to Britain forthwith. So that is that, get what belongings you have and meet in the courtyard in an hour." Yochana felt sick to the pit of my stomach. As she stood in the courtyard they could hear gun fire. It seemed like it was all round them. The first to get in the lorries to leave were the sick and the elderly. The Captain said the soldiers would be next, then the nursing staff and finally the helpers which Yochana was classed as.

THE HURT OF YOCHANA

The round trip to the harbour took about ninety minutes to unload the lorries. Finally it would be Yochana's turn. There was Yochana, two other women and three men. They waited and by now it was getting dark and cold. They huddled together to keep warm and still they waited. Eventually one of the men said, "they are not coming back for us are they?" Suddenly we could hear German voices. They burst into the courtyard killing two of the men who put up resistance. They pointed at the third man and told him to get Yochana and the other women into the back of one of the lorries. Yochana heard a German soldier say the word death camp. She shuddered, she had come so close to freedom and now this. She sat in the back of the wagon, the other woman and man were crying. I can't let

THE HURT OF
YOCHANA

them beat me She thought I must be strong. They arrived in a small town the sign said Sonzeen. There was a terrible stench in the air. They were herded like animals and taken through a set of grand looking iron gates across the top it simply said in German Herzlich Willkommen auf Sonzeen Arbeit ist der Weg zum Glück which translated in English was "Welcome to Sonzeen Work Is The Road to Happiness." Yochana knew what this was and also knew that this was probably the end of the road for her. The woman was still crying and the soldier simply pulled out his gun and said, "shut up Jewish whore." He said it twice and when she didn't, he shot her. She fell on the floor and he beckoned Yochana and the man to pick up her body. They carried it through the gates where an emaciated man in a striped suit was waiting with a wheel barrow to take the body away. Yochana was by now desensitised by all the death she had seen so she just carried on. They hosed them down and cut their hair and she was allocated a bunk in Shed G Number three.

Yochana wasn't feeling anything; fear, unhappiness, love, hate, absolutely nothing. She just felt numb as she entered this smelly rat hole that was now her home. As she walked down to her allocated bunk thin arms came from everywhere clawing at her. She looked the healthiest which she was hoping might save her life. The soldier barked at her that she was in the boot factory at 4.30am and to be by her bunk ready. She said, "thank you." He looked at her as if she was a nut job and she really didn't know why she

THE HURT OF
YOCHANA

said thank you. There was nothing to
thank these bastards for. Surprisingly she
slept ok, although bitten by all the fleas
and the smell was nauseating to say the
least.

They were all standing by their bunks at
the time they were told to be ready for
work, 4.30am. They were then marched
about a half mile through thick mud. On
the way two old women fell down and
were shot, and the man with the wheel
barrow who followed them every day
would take the bodies away. The biggest
shock was the first day Yochana sat at the
machine making the back of the leather
boots and next to her was vacant. She kept
her head down and worked. That way she
hoped she would not be chosen to be
murdered because she knew that's what
they did. About three hours after Yochana

THE HURT OF YOCHANA

started a woman came and sat down and started running the machine. Although they dare not talk they both lifted their heads and their eyes met. It was Astera. She looked at Yochana as if to say don't speak. The guards were up and down the line watching for any conversation. If you lifted your head they would pull you off the machine by your hair and hit you repeatedly with a stick. Yochana saw two women whipped to death for smiling at each other so she knew not to look or show emotion, but she couldn't wait to find out what happened, as she thought Astera had got away.

Just by luck, or maybe bad luck for the poor wretch who died in the bunk below, but Astera was allocated that bunk that very same night. Yochana sat on the bed that night and they talked and talked.

THE HURT OF
YOCHANA

Astera said the night she left Magadha the convoy the lorry carrying people went down a track in a small forest it appeared for no reason. The driver, who was French, told them to get out, and from nowhere German soldiers arrived. The driver thought he was safe, having clearly done what he was told, but one of the soldiers calmly walked up to him and shot him at point blank range. Astera thought this was the end for them all, but they calmly said to get back in the truck and they ended up here.

"Because we were well fed and fit, they needed us for the work Yochana," Astera said.

After talking for a long time in a quiet way they made a pact that they would get through this together and no matter what they would survive. The key to this was to stay under the radar do as they were told. Never look at the Germans and work hard, that way they figured they might survive.

Six months had passed when Yochana overheard a conversation between two German guards. They both seemed worried, one was saying that he never hurt a Jew but just did what he was told. The other said they will never let them live with the Americans only forty miles away. He had heard that they would all be shot and the camp raised to the ground, with all evidence destroyed.

Yochana told Astera what she had heard and they hatched a plan. They decided that once the killings started they would make a break for it. It was their only chance. The following morning they were

THE HURT OF
YOCHANA

assembled in the courtyard. The whole
place smelt of death. Yochana looked
around. Out of around six hundred people,
at best there were a hundred who like
Yochana and Astera looked fit.

The commandant arrived. He ordered
three Kapos to go amongst the massed
prisoners and pull out the weak. It didn't
matter if it was boy or girl. When they got
to Yochana and Astera they smirked but
didn't pull them out. Their hearts were
racing. They stood in the cold and watched
as approximately fifty at a time of the
weaker prisoners were taken away. The
stench arrived in the air, it made me feel
sick. I thought to myself I will never
forget that smell. After about eight hours
and with the snow falling there was about
a hundred of them left. They were herded
together and told they were going to work

at a nicer place. Astera griped Yochana's hand. Knowing how the Germans worked, Yochana thought they would be taken to the forest and shot. But this was not what happened. They were told to follow the lead Kapo. Yochana could see his horrible face and the green triangle he wore. Yochana thought, I hope one day your people who you have betrayed find you and you have to pay for your crimes.

They had been walking about fourteen hours and it was dark. Some that had fallen down in the cold were shot where they fell and left like dogs. Astera and Yochana stuck to what they had said and just walked. They thanked the few guards that were on the journey when they threw stale bread to them and they never looked at them. During the walk they could see a massive fire taking place which looked

THE HURT OF
YOCHANA

like the camp. Although they could not
hear any gun fire they hoped the
Americans had got there. The Guards said
they could stop and sleep before
continuing the march at day break.

Yochana listened at what the guards
were saying and they seemed worried.
Apparently they were being taken to
Germany. One guard actually said it was a
lost cause and they should shoot them and
make a run for it. If they needed the toilet,
a Kapo would take the prisoner. Astera
asked to go to the toilet and the Kapo who
they had called Pig face because of his big
nostrils grabbed her hand and took her to
the woods. Almost everyone was asleep. A
couple of minutes had passed and Astera
hadn't returned. Yochana took the chance
because she knew something was wrong.
As she got into the woods she could see

THE HURT OF
YOCHANA

Pig Face pulling his trousers down and Astera sobbing on the forest floor. He was about to rape her. She very quietly crept up behind him just as he was about to take poor Astera. She remembered how to break a neck which she did. The nasty pig fell on the ground in the thick snow which now carpeted the forest floor. They had to run for it. Yochana grabbed a knife that he had been given by the Germans.

Yochana was hoping that by the time he was discovered the Germans did not have the resource to hunt of for them and they would just carry on with the march.

Astera kept thanking Yochana, who told her there was nothing to thank her for. They could be in a worse mess. Yochana remembered the stars and how to navigate. She told Astera that they had to run and get about five miles away, then hide until the following night.

They had to find a place to stay. They were both so cold and took turns to wear the Kapo's jacket. It wasn't much but it did help. Their next job was food. They were so hungry they used the snow for refreshment.

"Jane, are you awake? Do you want some breakfast?"

Jane woke from her dream. She felt cold although the heating was on and she had an ample duvet on her bed.

"I will be a few minutes," she shouted as she scribbled down what had happened during the night.

"Do I tell Aunty Millie or do I act normal. I just don't want to worry her," she said to herself.

THE HURT OF YOCHANA

Jane sat at the kitchen table.

"Did you sleep well Jane?"

Although she hated lying, protecting Aunty Millie was more important Jane thought.

"Yes, had good night's sleep Aunty Millie."

"Good sweetheart, I have done you a boiled egg and some soldiers." The word soldier sent a shiver down Jane's spine as she thought of what Yochana and Astera were going through.

"Oh, thank you."

"There you go sweetheart enjoy that, then we can get off to see Nicola Gielbert."

It was 11.00 am when they arrived at the practice. The receptionist showed Millie and Jane into the surgery. Nicola Gielbert as usual was dressed immaculately with the French style that seemed to come so naturally. She wore a white blouse with a black cropped cardigan, a black pencil skirt which was just above her knee and pair of black and white Christian Louboutin shoes with their distinctive red soles.

Nicola greeted them both and asked if they would like a coffee before the regression or after. Jane opted for after. "Ok Jane please lie on the bed." Gielbert put some soothing music and slowly regressed Jane.

"Where are you now Jane?" At first Jane didn't respond so Nicola tried again.

"Where are you now Jane?"

"We are hiding, don't make a noise," Jane said.

"I will talk quietly. I want to ask you about the rose?"

THE HURT OF
YOCHANA

"What about the rose?"

"What does the rose mean to you?"

"My friend Astera gave me the rose, she is my friend."

"Is Astera with you?"

"Yes, why do you keep asking me these questions? Who are you?"

"I am your friend Jane. Jane I want to ask you about a lady called Maria?"

"I don't know anybody called Maria?"

"Does Astera know anybody called Maria?" Yochana paused for a minute.

"Maria is Astera's sister. Do you know where she is?"

"No I don't Yochana."

"Is she alive?"

"I don't know that either Yochana."

"Have you got food for me?"

"I'm sorry Yochana, no."

"Where are you?"

THE HURT OF YOCHANA

"We are under a bush waiting in the forest waiting for nightfall."

"Be careful Yochana."

"Who are you? I don't want to talk to you anymore. You are a German spy aren't you?"

Nicola gestured to Millie and she took her over to her desk.

"Jane is having a near real life experience. It is my opinion that she could be two people; one when she is awake and one when she is asleep. What we have to ensure is the sleeping Jane doesn't encroach and the real-life Jane, which is what happened to Mr. Egan. I think at the minute the regressed Jane is hungry and fretful. I don't think it would be wise to carry on today, maybe leave it for a few days until the sleeping Jane is more able to talk. I am frightened she won't trust me and then I won't be able to connect with her under regression."

"Is Jane ok Nicola?"

"She is very troubled Mrs. Egan and this is a fine balancing act. It is truly amazing what I am hearing this is something our profession doesn't see that often. I have looked very deeply into this and other than Mr. Egan, there was one reported case. A Mr. Litton from Morecambe in Lancashire he was the first and only reported case before Mr. Egan that was written down."

"What happened to him Nicola? Is Jane ok there?"

"Yes, she is just in a deep sleep."

"So Mr. Litton?"

"Yes, Harold Litton had been a World War Two Battle of Britain pilot and in September 1962 he started having dreams that were vivid like Liam and Jane's. I

have only found out about this yesterday.
You have to remember that regression was
very much in its infancy in 1962 nobody
took it seriously.

Harold Litton's dreams which started in
September 1962 and got so bad that in
March 1963, in sheer desperation he
contacted a Mr. Fielding. Fielding agreed
to put him into a regression program over
the coming months. Harold told Fielding
his story under regression. Harold said he
shot Abraham Lincoln. He said he was
John Wilkes Booth. Harold said he was a
stage actor but he wanted to revive the
Confederacy. He said initially he wasn't
the one that was going to do the deed. It
was going to be Lee Powell, but they
decided that Wilkes Booth would have a
better chance in the theatre with his acting
credentials. He said the decision was taken

that he would kill Lincoln, Powell and David Herold were assigned to kill the Secretary of State, William H Seward. The other conspirator George Atzerodt, was assigned to kill the Vice President Andrew Johnson. Harold told the story under regression how the others failed but he was successful. He said he shot Lincoln from behind in the head as he was watching the show, and he died in Petersen hospital.

Harold said he managed to get away but was eventually caught and killed. Because this was early days of regression nobody believed Fielding or Harold, they said the story was there for all to read.

When Harold died, Fielding, by now an old man, reported other things Harold had said. He said he had seen the real person that shot JFK and it wasn't Oswald. He

THE HURT OF
YOCHANA

said Harold died under regression in 1968,
still very troubled, as he seemed to have
been in or a party to some historical
happenings in the world.

The last two things that came to life
long after both Fielding and Harold Litton
had died, was he had said he was a
fireman in the Twin Towers helping after
the planes struck. It was like he was seeing
a future life, which isn't regression, so
Fielding never reported it to anyone for a
fear of ridicule to our profession. He also
said the actual word ISIS and said they
would rise in 2000 to try and dominate the
world in their image.

I am telling you this Millie because
Harold Litton said his life had changed in
September 1962. Although he had no
children he said he had been told in a
dream that in the future another boy would

carry the burden, and that his name was Daniel."

Millie's whole body ran cold.

"What are you telling me that Daniel is some kind of soothsayer Nicola?"

"I am sorry Millie but all these things are adding up."

"Harold Litton could have just been guessing."

"Yes, he could and you can see why Fielding didn't want to publish his findings. Although you have lived through this nightmare first with Mr. Egan, and now with Jane, you don't want to believe. People don't want to believe. Regression is quite often ridiculed as you know."

"Do you think I should tell Jane what you have told me Nicola?"

"Definitely not. Jane is fragile in her dream world already, and until we can make her mind want to live in the real world she is vulnerable. Right let's get Jane back with us."

"Jane, Jane come back to me," Nicola said stroking Jane's hand. Slowly Jane woke.

"Are you ok sweetheart?"

"I think so Aunty Millie. Did I say anything?"

"Nicola is making us a coffee, then she will tell you her findings." Nicola came back with three coffees and biscotti with each drink.

"How do you feel Jane?" said Nicola.

"Ok I think. What did I say?"

"Well I am trying to get to the bottom of the significance of the rose."

Nicola explained about Astera. Jane didn't say anything but decided when she went to Liverpool she was going to take a proper look in the loft at the café.

"I think it would be best Jane, if we did the next session next Tuesday."

"Yes, that's fine Nicola. I am going to stay with my friend in Liverpool at the weekend so won't be back until after lunch on Monday."

"Ok well enjoy your break." The girls finished the coffee and Nicola showed them out.

"What would you like to do now Jane?"

"Shall we go to Camden Lock for some late lunch?"

"Yes, let's I haven't been there for ages. Me and Jamie used to often go on Sunday before it was as popular as it is now. Millie hailed a taxi and it dropped them at Willie McFee's Beautiful Food. McFee had been a top chef and was on the TV all the time. Then one day he dropped out and bought a small transport café. It became a legend in Camden. Jane told Millie that McFee would quite often serve the customers, as well as cook.

McFee's was painted a lilac colour on the outside, with a door that had a bell like in the old post offices, that let you know when somebody entered. All the tables had lilac table cloths with small thistle motifs embroidered on them, A young Scottish girl seated them in the window and handed them the menus. They both ordered a coffee and the menu whilst not extensive, was acceptable. The food came out looked amazing. Jane ordered the McFee Philly Cheese Steak and Millie ordered McFee Frittata. Both meals arrived in a timely manner and looked tremendous. The Philly Cheese Steak was not your run of the mill Philly cheese steak. This had aged rib eye with foie-gras and topped with homemade fontina cheese on a sesame roll. It was accompanied by a small glass of Dom Perignon. Millie's dish the Frittata had half a pound of lobster and an ounce of caviar on a bed of crocked sweet potato.

It was almost six o clock when they paid and hailed a taxi home. Jane cuddled onto Millie.

"That was so nice Aunty Millie, I love having this time with you."

"I do too sweetheart," Millie said. Once back in the house they sat looking at old pictures with a glass of brandy and Baileys each. It was almost ten o clock when they decided enough was enough.

THE HURT OF
YOCHANA

"What time is your train to Liverpool in the morning Jane?"

"11.10am leaving St Pancras."

"Is Jenny meeting you in Liverpool?"

"Yeah, I can't wait to see her Aunty Millie."

"I am sure the feeling will be mutual Jane. Goodnight sweetheart."

"Good night Aunty Millie and thank you for a fantastic day." Jane went to her room and packed her small suitcase. She made sure the diary was the first thing in there.

Jane was soon asleep but she didn't dream and the next day felt quite fresh as Millie dropped her at the train station. Once Millie was back in her house she decided to look up Harold Litton and Fielding. There was a surprising amount of information about his story and his dreams and predictions. Nothing more than what Nicola Gielbert had told her, but there was no mention of a Daniel which she was a little surprised at.

Meanwhile Jane had arrived in Liverpool and was meeting Jenny. They knew each other straight away and ran and embraced like long lost sisters.

"Come on," Jane said, "let's go and have a coffee. We have so much catching up to do." Starbucks was just outside the station. Jane ordered a couple of coffees but wanted to give Jenny her surprise about Ringo's. They sat just talking and laughing, then Jane showed Jenny the deeds, and that Ringo's was now hers to do as she wished.

Jenny broke down, "Oh Jane, I have been so worried that you might say you were selling the café."

THE HURT OF
YOCHANA

"Jenny, don't be daft. You are my best friend, I wouldn't do that to you, I owe you so much." As they sat talking Jane felt a tap on her shoulder.

"Well if it isn't Jane Egan and Jenny Makepeace. How are you girls?" Jane's heart was racing. It was Matt Babbington, father of Daniel, although he didn't know. Both girls were like rabbits in a car's headlights.

"What are you doing back in Liverpool?"

Jenny quickly said visiting. She didn't want Matt to know about the café.

"I heard you had been poorly Jane, and you both dropped out of University. Somebody said meningitis. Was that correct." Jane said yes, the sooner she could get rid of him the better. Trouble was Matt wasn't for going and pulled up a chair.

"So where do you both live now?"

Jane said she lived in Herefordshire and Jenny said she lived in Wales.

"Both married farmers I bet." Both girls just smiled.

"What about children?" Jane felt nervous, though she hadn't seen Matt for years she could see such a resemblance in Daniel. Jenny realised he was prying so took up the conversation.

"So did Matt Babbington get into Politics then?"

"No, I'm afraid I didn't I passed my second year. Then my father was taken ill, so I left Liverpool to help my mother with the estate."

"Are you married then Matt?"

THE HURT OF YOCHANA

"Divorced with two children; one boy and a girl. They live with their mother in LA."

"What about your friend Simon?"

"To be honest Simon got into some real nasty shit, that's why I was glad to go home. We have never seen each other since. Somebody did tell me about five years ago that he was in some hell hole prison in Thailand, but I don't know if that is true or not."

"Why are you in Liverpool then?"

"Just here for the weekend. I run part of the estate as a high-class hotel and one of my suppliers asked me up for a golf weekend, so I thought why not. Listen do you fancy meeting at Ringo's Saturday morning for a coffee and a piece of that Jewish cheesecake, that's if it's still there of course?"

THE HURT OF
YOCHANA

Jane replied, "We have a lot on Matt and only the weekend to cram it all in."

"Well look here is my card. Ring me tonight if you can make it. It's been really nice to see you both," and he got up gave them both a peck on the cheek and left. He was still a stunning looking man.

"What do we do now?

"Shut the bloody café for the weekend and then if he does turn up he will never know Jen."

"He is still good looking isn't he Jen?"

"Don't go there Jane Egan, he caused you enough grief back in the day."

"Daniel looks so much like him. I don't know if I am doing the right thing not telling him."

"Has Daniel asked you who is father is Jane?"

THE HURT OF
YOCHANA

"No, he hasn't yet. I have been dreading the day he does to be honest. At least having seen Matt again he appears to have grown up." The girls finished their coffees and paid.

"Come on let's go back to mine. It seems so strange saying mine."

Back at the café Jenny showed Jane a picture of the girls, Bridie and Clodagh.

"What pretty girls. Where are they? Can't wait to meet them Jen."

"They are twin girls Jen, and are both on a school trip to Rome for four days. My husband who you can guess is Irish. He is back home visiting his Ma who is very poorly."

"What's his name Jen?"

"Promise you won't laugh."

"I promise."

"It's Dump."

THE HURT OF
YOCHANA

"Dump, what like when you go to the toilet?" both girls were laughing.

"Well yeah, his full name is Dump Dermot Kennedy."

"Do you call him Dump, Jen?"

"Yeah, that's his name. His dad, his granddad, and his great granddad were all called Dump." This set Jane off laughing again.

"Oh, I have missed you mate."

"Missed you too Jane Egan."

"Do you still have all my things in the loft Jen?"

"Yeah I do, but I don't go there. Look I have to tell you Clodagh was in the loft and came across your things. Being a kid she had to look. She saw the rose and the vase and said she saw a little old lady who said "They must pay". She was so frightened Jane.

THE HURT OF
YOCHANA

"It would have been Maria Klinck, I am sure Jen. Aunty Millie has taken me to a Regression specialist because they think if I can find the significance of the Rose that Maria gave me, then the dreams will stop."

"Is it working?"

"Well I have only been a couple of times but the dreams seem to have slowed down to be honest."

"Oh let's hope so Jane, so you can have a normal life." That night Jane went into the loft. Jenny said she was too scared.

The boxes of personal things were exactly how she had left them. She dusted off a few things and in the bottom of one box was a small diary. It was Maria Klincks. She sat cross legged reading it. In it Maria had written a date 'February 3rd

THE HURT OF
YOCHANA

1945. This day I will always be grateful to Yochana for saving my sister.'

Maria Klinck then went on to say she would not meet Yochana until just before she died. This sent a shiver down Jane's spine. She had then written about her life but mentioned many times that Yochana would come and see her one day. She then said after Yochana has lived her dream she will…. the next three pages had been ripped out to give no ending.

Jane's heart was racing when Jenny shouted up, "Are you ok Jane?"

Jane replied all buoyant, "Yes I'm fine. I will be down in a bit." Jane carried on looking through old pictures of Maria, then she came across one of Astera. She knew it was her as she remembered the little mole that Astera had almost identical

THE HURT OF
YOCHANA

to Marilyn Monroe's. They were both pretty girls. At the bottom of one box was a tattered card but on it somebody had drawn a set of beautiful roses clustered round a quote which simply said

"A rose will wait for you when time will not. A rose will give you comfort when a being will not. All those people that want to hurt you, it will never be the rose that hurts you. Remember your rose has thorns but your rose also has beauty and if you hurt your rose, your rose and its thorns will hurt you. Because everybody has to pay for what they do in the garden of life and the rose will protect you. The day will come when your rose can no longer protect you but on that day you will know they paid for what they did"

Maria Chayobbi

THE HURT OF YOCHANA

Was this the answer to the dreams, but what did she mean that one day the rose would not protect her? Did that mean the end? She brought the card and the small diary of Maria's down from the loft and she phoned Millie so that she could tell Nicola Gielbert. Millie tried to be upbeat but something was nagging at her, this all sounded so sinister.

As soon as Jane was off the phone she phoned Nicola Gielbert. Nicola listened without commenting, "I don't think this is something we can talk about over the phone Mrs. Trench. Meet me for a coffee at my practice in the morning so we can discuss." Jane agreed to be at the practice at 10.30am the following day. Meanwhile Jane was telling Jenny about what she found and she was writing in her diary at the same time. It was almost like she was

THE HURT OF
YOCHANA

possessed Jenny thought. She was scared for her friend as she could see this was taking over yet again.

That night Jane's mind was buzzing as she fell asleep. Yochana almost immediately took over. It was dark in the distance they could see lights so maybe a town. They could hear gun-fire all around them. With their stomachs empty they had to get food so they took the chance and walked towards the lights. They could see that the side of the hill they were on was being defended by American and British troops. They got close to some barrack like buildings when suddenly they were surrounded by soldiers. Yochana tried to explain but they clearly thought the girls were some kind of German spies.

THE HURT OF
YOCHANA

Yochana and Astera were ushered into a room where a British officer sat behind a desk, either side of him were two burly soldiers. The British officers started asking the questions. After almost an hour Astera fainted from the hunger, so they arranged for some meat and bread to be brought in.

Eventually it appeared the officer believed their story as he knew of Magadha and Captain Nichol.

"Ok we will get you some warm clothes and I will send two soldiers with you to get you home. This is not without risk you must understand this." Both girls nodded in agreement and the following morning they climbed on the back of two motorbikes with the two British soldiers and headed out.

THE HURT OF YOCHANA

It was three days later when they arrived
near the coastal town of Amiloes. The
soldiers said there were British boats in
the harbour that would get them to Great
Britain and safety. They told them it was a
three mile walk and to go at nightfall as
there were pockets of German resistance
still roaming Amiloes. The girls thanked
the soldiers and hid until it was early
morning. Then they headed towards the
harbour. After almost two miles Astera
stopped, she had a stone in her shoe.
From out of darkened side street came a
German soldier. Yochana could see he
was injured and she could also see the
glint of the knife in his hand. Yochana
pushed Astera over and grappled with the
lone soldier. Although he was injured he
was still stronger than Yochana. He
pushed the knife into Yochana's side. As

THE HURT OF
YOCHANA

he did this Yochana rolled to one side, grabbed a large stone, and hit the soldier square between the eyes. He fell on his side. Yochana was bleeding profusely but she knew the soldier wasn't dead. She also knew pulling the knife out of her would possibly mean her death. She didn't hesitate, she pulled knife and plunged it into the heart of the German soldier then fell back exhausted. Two British soldiers on hearing the commotion came running out of the shadows but it was too late Yochana's courage had saved Astera at the cost of her own life.

Jane woke up. The rose was on the floor and the vase was smashed. Jenny came in half asleep and saw the mess. Jane was sitting up in bed crying. Jenny consoled her and Jane told her what had happened.

THE HURT OF
YOCHANA

"Jane maybe this is the end of this for you." Or the beginning Jane thought.

Jane never had another dream and almost three years had passed. Daniel was now an adult and at University in Cambridge, studying history. Millie had taken early retirement and Jane, who was quite a rich woman, just enjoyed seeing Jenny and going on holidays with Millie. They never went back to Nicola Gielbert's practice again.

It wasn't until Jane got involved in selling poppies for the British Legion and she climbed the ladder and became a high-ranking member of the organization. It was now four years since the last dream and the death of Yochana. Jane had tried unsuccessfully to find Astera but to no avail. Then one day she saw on one of the

THE HURT OF
YOCHANA

Legion sites that they were running a trip
to France to the war graves and it was near
Amiloes. Millie didn't think it was a good
idea but Jane was adamant she was going.
Millie couldn't let her go on her own so
she went along with her.

The trip arrived at the war graves. As
usual Jane had been looking at her diary
and she knew it was on the same day of
her last dream. They wandered between
the white crosses in the neatly lawned
cemetery. Millie knew Jane was looking
for Yochana's grave. At grave number 336
they found a cross which simply said 'A
brave woman Yochana,' and the date of
her death. Jane reached into her bag and
took out the rose that Maria Klinck had
given her all those years ago and placed it
on the tombstone.

THE HURT OF YOCHANA

Everything made sense now and closure was given. Jane and Millie stood in silence, eyes closed both saying a prayer. Eventually the coach organiser asked them to all get back on the coach as they were staying overnight in Amiloes. The little hotel was very neat and tidy. The French hosts were very kind and accommodating, telling the visitors about the war years and how they wanted to thank the British for saving them.

There were six tables of eight people for supper. On Jane and Millie's table were two old soldiers whose brother was buried at the cemetery, and two school teachers who said they were on a fact-finding mission for a school course. Then a man and women who both appeared to be in their nineties. They didn't say anything throughout the meal. Eventually everyone had gone to bed except Millie and Jane and the old couple on their table. Jane asked them their names. The man said his name was Arthur. Jane looked at the woman for an answer. She looked Jane straight in the eyes and said, "you know who I am?" Jane looked at Millie.

"I'm sorry, do I know you?"

"Why are you here today?" Jane gave a very small version of the reason that she wanted to find Yochana's grave, if indeed it existed. Suddenly the woman got up and shuffled towards Jane.

"Thank you my dear. Maria said one day I would meet you."

"Maria?" Jane said.

"Yes my sister, I am Astera and I have lived for this moment all my life." Jane was lost for words. The old lady said, "it is

.

now time for me to go. I bless you my dear." Astera and Arthur left the table.

Jane looked at Millie, "I can't remember seeing them on the coach trip."

They called the trip co-coordinator over.

"The couple sitting on our table, Astera and Arthur where are they from?"

The lady looked a bit shocked.

"I'm sorry, I don't have an Astera and Arthur on your table, only had six people. You and Mrs. Trench, Mrs. Young and Mrs. King the teachers, and Mr. Preston and Mr. Kinder the ex-soldiers."

Both Millie and Jane were shocked at this revelation. The following morning over breakfast they asked the other people who had sat with them the night before about Arthur and Astera, and they looked at them as if they had gone out of their minds.

THE HURT OF
YOCHANA

With Millie and Jane totally bemused they set off back to England. Jane lived now at a house across the road from Millie. They were both dropped off. The following morning Millie called round to make sure Jane was ok. Strangely the front door was open. She shouted, "Jane," but there was no answer so she made her way up the stairs.

Jane was lying on the bed with her diary, on the last page. She had finished writing it. On the last page she had written 'Aunty Millie please look after Daniel.'

Jane was dead but is this the end of the nightmare for the Egan family or is Daniel about to be plunged into a different world? Would the church in Paisley hold all the answers?

The End

THE HURT OF YOCHANA

Current list of books by Colin J Galtrey

The John Gammon Detective Series

Series One

Book One: Things Will Never Be The Same Again

Book Two: Sad Man

Book Three: Joy Follows Sorrow

Book Four: Never Cry On A Bluebell

Book Five: Annie Tanney

Series Two

Book One: The Poet And The Calling Card

Book Two: Why

Historical Time Travel Series

Book One: Looking For Shona

Book Two: The Hurt of Yochana

Thriller

Got To Keep Running

THE HURT OF
YOCHANA

Sample reviews of my previous books

Got To Keep Running: Available in Kindle /Paperback and Audio on Amazon. Audio also available on Audible.Com and I Tunes

> ⭐⭐⭐⭐⭐ Five Stars
> Excellent read. Now reading Sad Man equally as gripping. Love the continuity of the characters.
> Sandra Hodgkinson
> Published 17 months ago by ANDY

Sad Man: Available on Kindle and Paperback on Amazon.

> ⭐⭐⭐⭐⭐ Another great story from Colin Galtrey.
> By MandoK on 25 August 2015
> Format: Kindle Edition | Verified Purchase
> Another gripping story in the John Gammon series, couldn't put it down, excellent read,

Joy Follows Sorrow: Available on Kindle and Paperback on Amazon

> ⭐⭐⭐⭐⭐ Must read
> By David Misell-mellor on 27 November 2015
> Format: Kindle Edition | Verified Purchase
> Great read from a great author

THE HURT OF YOCHANA

Never Cry On A Bluebell: Available on Kindle and Paperback on Amazon

⭐⭐⭐⭐⭐ **Leaves you wanting more!**
By michelle on 2 March 2016
Format: Paperback | Verified Purchase

What an ending!!mr galtrey you had better have started the sequel .
Read this book in three days best one yet!

Annie Tanney: Available on Kindle and Paperback on Amazon

⭐⭐⭐⭐☆ **Four Stars**
By Doreen Markham on 15 July 2016
Format: Kindle Edition | Verified Purchase

Yet again another brill book could not put it down made me cry

The Poet and the Calling Card: Available on Kindle and Paperback on Amazon

⭐⭐⭐⭐⭐ Excellent
By Amazon Customer on 23 December 2016
Format: Kindle Edition | Verified Purchase

Brilliant book again cannot wait to start next book to find out the reason why looking forward to another good read

THE HURT OF
YOCHANA

WHY: Available on Kindle and Paperback on Amazon

☆☆☆☆☆ I love the John Gammon books
By JHL on 15 December 2016
Verified Purchase

Exceptional storyline, I love the John Gammon books, they leave me feeling like I know the characters personally.

Got To Keep Running: Available on Kindle and Paperback on Amazon

☆☆☆☆☆ Five Stars
By Amazon Customer on 21 November 2016
Format: Paperback | Verified Purchase

Excellent read couldn't put the book down

Looking For Shona: Available on Kindle and Paperback on Amazon now also available on BookBub.

☆☆☆☆☆ Five Stars
By Amazon Customer on 29 October 2016
Format: Paperback | Verified Purchase

Brilliant writing keeps one wondering until last page bring on some more

Printed in Germany
by Amazon Distribution
GmbH, Leipzig

17212048R00235